PRAISE FOR JOHAN HARSTAD

.

"Like Jonathan Safran Foer, Harstad combines formal play and linguistic ferocity with a searing emotional directness."—Dedi Felman, *Words Without Borders*

"The fact is that Johan Harstad has a wholly unique voice, simultaneously both concrete and soaring . . . to be able to write in this way, to conjure a situation and construct space and time around it with such linguistic fluency, cannot be learned. You are born with it."—Jakob Levinsen, *Jyllands-Posten review*

"As entertaining as it is astute, and as amusing as it is melancholic. . . . Have we ever read a book that deals with so much, has such high aims and works with so many references to art, theatre, literature and film, all without failing?"—*Berliner Zeitung*

"This paradoxical desire to be seen without being heralded sets [*Buzz Aldrin, What Happened to You in All the Confusion?*'s] hero apart from other tormented young men of contemporary literature . . . [an] ambitious debut."
—*Publisher's Weekly*

"The austere landscape and people of the Faeroes become players in Harstad's [*Buzz Aldrin, What Happened to You in All the Confusion?*], half-dramatic and half-comic, which takes on memorable turns with every page as Mattias realizes just how not in control of his destiny he really is. A modern saga of rocketships, ice floes and dreams of the Caribbean, and great fun to read."
—*Kirkus Reviews*

The Red Handler
Collected Works
ANNOTATED EDITION

A Novel

Johan Harstad

TRANSLATED BY DAVID M. SMITH

OPEN LETTER
LITERARY TRANSLATIONS FROM THE UNIVERSITY OF ROCHESTER

Originally published in Norwegian as *Ferskenen* by Gyldendal Norsk Forlag
Copyright © 2018 by Johan Harstad
Translation copyright © 2023 by David M. Smith

BASED ON AN IDEA FROM ARILD ØSTIN OMMUNDSEN

First edition, 2023

Library of Congress Cataloging-in-Publication Data: Available

ISBN (pb): 978-1-948830-80-5
ISBN (ebook): 978-1-948830-93-5

*This project is supported in part by an award from the New York State Council on the Arts with the
support of the governor of New York and the New York State Legislature*

Printed on acid-free paper in the United States of America.

Cover Design by Luke Bird
Photo © Studio Firma/Stocksy; (gun) © Michal Boubin / Alamy;
(blood) © merahn saeed / Alamy

Open Letter is the University of Rochester's nonprofit, literary translation press:
Lattimore Hall 411, Box 270082, Rochester, NY 14627

www.openletterbooks.org

The Red Handler
Collected Works
ANNOTATED EDITION

A Novel

That there

That's not me

BIOGRAPHY

Frode Brandeggen (1970-2014) was born in Stavanger, Norway and grew up in the neighborhood of Tjensvoll. An only child, Brandeggen soon took a liking to literature and wrote his first short story at the young age of eleven, the thirteen-page "Knutsen Finds Something Exciting in the Garden." The text, written in a careful cursive and given its own painstakingly decorated title page, was unfortunately thrown out by his father during a fit of rage and was therefore never read by anyone. Brandeggen's first publication came in 1990 in the literary zine *Kakofoni*, a short story entitled "An Anomaly," written during his studies at the University of Oslo. Two years later, his avant-garde debut novel, *Conglomeratic Breath*, was published by Gyldendal Norsk Forlag. As a result of its forbidding length and complexity, *Conglomeratic Breath* was ignored by reviewers and quickly forgotten. It sold poorly, and is nearly impossible to find today in any bookshop or antiquarian bookseller. Gyldendal destroyed all remaindered copies in the autumn of 1993.

The year following this disappointing debut, Brandeggen moved back to Stavanger and worked at various odd jobs, including garbage collection, while tenaciously (though in secret) working to develop a new way of writing, one that would enable him to realize his own artistic potential while also appealing to a wider audience. The result was a fifteen-book series featuring a private detective called the Red Handler; written in a kind of micronovelistic form inspired by the French *Mouvement artistique du banalisme*, a literary movement that championed anticlimax, cliché, and omission as worthy literary techniques. The novels were never submitted to Gyldendal or any other Norwegian publisher.

Frode Brandeggen died from emaciation in his Stavanger apartment in the autumn of 2014.

His novels are collected for the first time in this posthumous edition, annotated by Brandeggen's German friend and professional annotator, Bruno Aigner (1934 –), who, in addition to his extensive knowledge of the author, has had the benefit of access to Brandeggen's papers.

CONTENTS

THE RED HANDLER HOT ON THE TRAIL

CHAPTER I

Rain-soaked streets. One of the town's lost souls flew past like a leaf in the wind.[1] In the old Opel with Haugesund plates sat the Red Handler, private detective. He took a gulp from a flask etched with the words, *To my dear husband.*[2] He envisioned his ex-wife for a brief second, before the liquor flushed the painful memory down the sewers of oblivion.[3] He turned on his car stereo. From the speakers flowed the tones of Glenn Gould's recording of the *Goldberg Variations.*[4] The later recording, the one from the 80s.

The Red Handler closed his eyes as the eminent piano tones played with his ears.

Suddenly, he heard a sound. He could see nothing. He opened his eyes. That helped.[5] Someone was trying to break into a house a little ways down the street.[6]

The Red Handler burst out of his vehicle. A short chase ensued. Then it was over. Before the thief could protest, the Red Handler had laid him out, smack on the ground.

"Now I've got you," whispered the Red Handler.

The thief knew at once the jig was up.[7]

CHAPTER 3

The weather had cleared. The city was safe once more.

The Red Handler lit a cigarette and got back into his car. After the divorce, this was his sole source of pleasure. To smoke in his own car, free from that bitch's constant sniping.[8]

He turned up his car stereo full-blast. From it came some sort of rumba melody.[9] That's just how it was sometimes.

THE RED HANDLER STUMBLES ACROSS IT

CHAPTER I

The clouds resembled coagulated blood.[10] For the public at large it was just another glorious summer day, but not for the Red Handler. For him it was the prelude to one more night in service to the people, among the town's seedy criminals.[11] The air was already thick with their misdeeds.

CHAPTER 2

He flew down the city's main thoroughfare with one goal—to buy a pack of mints before the evening got underway—when suddenly he felt himself lose balance;[12] both feet left the ground, while the rest of his body seemed to hang in the air a second or two, before he came down hard on the gray asphalt with an audible smack.

He had stumbled.[13] Turning over on his side, he caught sight of the perpetrator: a hole in the pavement where someone or something had smashed the concrete to bits. "I'll be damned if this town isn't falling apart," he thought to himself, bitterly.

His left knee was throbbing. Most people would've applied a cold compress, checked for anything broken. But not the Red Handler. To him pain was nothing more than weakness leaving the body.[14]

He was about to get up when an open basement window only a half meter from his face caught his attention. Inside, a killer was bent over his victim, laughing.

With perfect disregard for his own safety, the Red Handler pushed himself up on his arms and legs and crawled in through the window. With a tiger's precision, he seized the killer's throat and pulled him down to the dirty basement floor.[15] A short fight ensued. Drama, too.[16] But under the onslaught of the Red

Handler's right hook and merciless jabs, the killer didn't stand a chance.[17]

"Now I've got you!" exclaimed the detective as he helped the killer to his feet so he could handcuff him.

"Dammit!" whispered the killer, most of all to himself.[18]

The Red Handler shook his head. He'd seen almost everything, but the sight of a life extinguished never lost its sting. He forced the killer to look at his victim.

"This is your deed, is it not?"

The killer hesitated as long as he dared. "You are too good, Red Handler. Yes . . ."

"That spells jail for you, mister. You'll be climbing the walls before they let you out of that joint. It's a good thing you admitted it, in any case. I'll make sure that goes down in the records. It might mean the difference between Alpha and Omega for you."

At this, the killer's face showed terror.

". . . and Omega? Are you sure?"

"I am," said the Red Handler gravely. "After alpha comes Omega.[19] That's how it works. You know, *causality.*"

"That's a hard word," sighed the murderer.

"It's a hard town," replied the Red Handler.

"I'll agree with you there."

"Come along."

The Red Handler laid a consoling arm around the murderer's shoulders as he led him out from the basement and into the inferno of the evening. They might've been on different sides of the law, but they were also two sides of the same coin.[20]

THE RED HANDLER AND
THE GLIMMER MAN

CHAPTER I

No one knew for certain where he was from. It was said he came from Haugesund, by car.[21] That he had a past. That he wasn't from Haugesund, but it was there he had burned all his bridges. Already that was long ago.[22] The person he was before no longer mattered.[23] Now he was the one forever catching murderers and crooks red-handed, just after dusk, through nights endless and strange, and the mysterious morning hours. He was the one who never gave up and never got tired. Now he was simply the Red Handler. The one who had come to watch over this city.[24]

The Red Handler put on his coat and picked up the keys that lay on today's newspaper in the hallway. "Murderer Caught *Red-Handler'ed* Last Night—Again!" The same headline, in some form or another, every day for the past few months. He left the paper where it was. He'd been there, no point reading about it, and something had to stay behind his eyes so the alcohol could wash it away. He took a sip. One was enough, had to stay sharp. There would be time to resume as soon as morning arrived. To drink, before slowly sliding into sleep and unconsciousness on the couch in front of the TV. Before starting all over again.[25]

He locked his apartment door and stepped into the street.[26]

On the other side of town, another man was doing the very same thing.[27] His keys lay on a newspaper with the same headline, but it wasn't about him, a fact of which he was all too aware. That'll all change after tonight, he told himself. The man locked the door to his enormous apartment and polished the brass name plate with the sleeve of his expensive designer suit: GLIMMER MAN, it read.[28] He'd installed it himself; no one else called him that.

Yet.

CHAPTER 3

In an opulent villa somewhere between the two men, in a part of town where neither of them could afford to live and had scarcely ever set foot, the beautiful woman let her negligée fall to the floor and positively floated into her walk-in closet, where she carefully chose an appropriate bathing suit and slid into it. She nonchalantly picked up a flirtini from the coffee table and strode out to the deck chairs by the swimming pool.[29] She threw herself into one of them and sipped her cocktail while resting her gaze upon the water. She must have nodded off shortly after, for she failed to notice the detective in his overcoat suddenly sitting in the chair next to hers.

She gave a start. "Oh my God, who are you?" she shouted.

The Red Handler stood up and looked out across the plot of land. "I think you know," he said with his back turned.

She nodded. He saw it. He had eyes on the back of his head.[30]

The Red Handler picked up her glass and studied it. "Flirtini, I presume?"[31]

"Is there anything you *don't* know?"

"Just this," he answered while looking straight at her. "Why are you lying here sunning yourself now?"

The woman shot him a sly grin. She wasn't the first to do that.

"Last time I checked, it wasn't a crime to sunbathe in one's own garden," she said sarcastically.

The Red Handler nodded.

"Very few, however, do it at three in the morning," he said calmly while taking a sip of the cocktail. Goddamn. She was beautiful, and if there was anything that could lead to trouble, it was that.

"I got a phone call," he continued, "of the concerned variety. A neighbor heard screams and gunfire from your residence."

"I don't know anything about it."

"No?"

"Nada."

The Red Handler grabbed her arm, which had to have hurt a little. She moaned.[32]

"And what about that?" he said sternly while pointing at the body floating face-down in the pool. The cool breeze stirred the deceased around in slow, red circles.

"Hmm?" She pretended as if she didn't quite understand what he was talking about. The woman stood up and downed the rest of the flirtini. She licked her lips.

"Oh, him? No, he was there when I got here."[33] Now it was her turn to grab the Red Handler's arm. "Why don't we go inside? I think I need a ..."

"Flirtini?"

"For one thing."

CHAPTER 4

Afterward, he wasn't proud of it. They'd gone to bed together. Everything had gone as it should. No problems in that department. He'd do it again if he had to. The whole thing had, as they say, whetted his appetite for more.[34]

CHAPTER 5

But he had a case to solve.[35]

He got out of bed and got dressed. While she was in the shower, he had a look around inside the villa.

Then he ran back to the bathroom, tore the shower curtain aside, and grabbed hold of the woman he'd just made love to. Made love to, yes, but never loved. If that was even something he could still do.

"You're coming with me to the station, Miss."

"Oh my God, what do you mean!?"

"I mean you're under arrest for the murder of your husband."

Most of all she seemed resigned, jaded. She put up no resistance.

"Jesus. At least let me get dressed first."

The Red Handler took off his coat and draped it over her.

"That'll do," he said with finality, while leading her through the rooms of the home.

She held her gaze down and asked: "How . . . how did you find me out, I . . ."

The Red Handler helped her into the backseat of the Opel and smiled laconically.

"I borrowed your computer for a moment while you were in the shower. Your search history revealed you had googled three topics repeatedly throughout the past week: 1) *How to murder your husband and make it look like someone else did it or even better like he's just gone for a swim*, 2) *How to clean a swimming pool*, and 3) *How to make a good flirtini in a heartbeat*."[36]

The woman shook her head quietly. "You are too good, Red Handler. Much too good."[37]

"You mean right now or a half-hour ago?" he replied, and swung the door shut before she could answer.[38]

CHAPTER 6

He sat behind the wheel and kept his eyes on the road in front of him as he drove down the avenue leading to the main road. The woman in the backseat was silent, she knew there was nothing she could say that could make him change his mind or deliver her from a lifetime behind bars. She'd never get her hands on her husband's stock portfolio, after all.[39]

The Red Handler turned onto the road with a practiced motion of the wheel.[40] Behind him a car swerved into the avenue he'd just exited, giving him just a glimmer of the driver before the latter pushed the pedal to the floor and tore toward the house where the body still swam in solitude. But he was too late.

The Red Handler kept his eyes on the rearview mirror for a moment. He couldn't say for sure who it had been, but nonetheless, he knew it instinctively.

"My nemesis," he thought to himself. "My nemesis."[41]

THE RED HANDLER AND
THE GREAT DIAMOND HEIST

CHAPTER I

His name was the Red Handler. He woke up to his cell phone emitting an abominable noise. It was ringing. Still half-asleep, he made a mental note to learn how to adjust the volume on that infernal gadget. But once he was fully awake, he saw his technological incompetence all too clearly. No one can do everything, he told himself. *But I can talk.*[42]

"Hello?" he spoke into the telephone.

A mysterious, raspy voice said, "Psst. A heist is underway at the diamond store down the street. Keep your eyes open."

"Who is this?"

"That doesn't matter. Just think of me as someone who wants to help."

Perhaps it was Bernt.[43] That would be just like him.

The mysterious caller hung up before the Red Handler could ask anything else.

CHAPTER 2

The Red Handler opened the drapes and looked out over the street. It was deserted this early in the morning. He shuffled into the kitchen, started the coffee, and took out the sandwich iron. He was a man who knew the value of a good breakfast.[44] While spreading orange marmalade on the toast, he thought of the words he'd heard from the mysterious voice. *Keep your eyes open.*[45] The Red Handler arranged his breakfast on a tray he'd gotten himself as a Christmas present and settled in beside the window. Right after his first sip of coffee,[46] he saw a person running down the street. The Red Handler stood up and yelled out to him: "Hey, you there! Stop!"

The person stopped and glanced nervously at the detective leaning out of the window in his bathrobe.[47]

"Are you the thief?" shouted the Red Handler.

"Nope," the person answered. "Sorry."[48]

The Red Handler had no choice but to let him go. A setback, no question. This would be a much harder case to crack than he'd thought.[49]

CHAPTER 3

He took a bite of the marmalade-covered slice of toast. He immediately started choking on it. *Help!* He couldn't breathe. Drama ensued.[50] The Red Handler was forced to wash it down with coffee. That made it better.[51] It was a close call.[52] He gave a relieved sigh, walked into the kitchen, and examined the sandwich iron closely. Just as he'd thought. He'd toasted the bread too long, burned it to a crisp.[53] Once again. Either that, or his aunt was after him.[54] She always had on a yellow dress when he met her.[55] That could only mean one thing. But there was nothing he could do about that today. There was a time for everything.

CHAPTER 4

Back by the window the Red Handler saw another person running down the street.

"Stop!" The birds flapped up from the rooftops when they
heard the Red Handler's voice ringing out.

The person stopped abruptly.

"Are you the diamond thief?" the Red Handler asked gravely.

The thief let go of his sack of loot and put up his hands.

"I can't deny it, no."[56]

"Just as I thought. You'd better bring that loot over here,
'cause you're under arrest."

"Dammit."

CHAPTER 5

The thief walked gloomily into the Red Handler's apartment.

"I'd offer you some breakfast," began the Red Handler, "but unfortunately, I'm out of dishwares. Or is it dishware?"

"I don't know," the thief replied with some embarrassment. "I guess I just thought it was dishes."[57]

"Let's not dwell on it," the Red Handler said sympathetically, pointing to an empty chair. "We'll just say plates.[58] And unfortunately I'm out of clean ones."

"That's all right, thanks," said the thief. "I ate before the robbery."[59]

"Smart. But that's the only smart thing you've done today. We'll head down to the station once I'm done eating. You'd better get ready to spend the next few years in the joint."[60]

The thief nodded his head slowly. Then they looked at each other across the table.

"Maybe I will have that cup of coffee, while I wait," said the thief.

The Red Handler folded his arms and studied the figure at the other end of the table.

"I'm out of clean cups, too," he answered, slowly.

But the thief didn't give up.

"A mug, maybe?"[61]

In one violent swoop the Red Handler cleared the entire table, sending the coffee, toast, marmalade, plate, and cup flying to the floor with a crash. He hadn't felt such rage since his aunt had given him that infernal sandwich press.[62]

They walked out into the brutal morning together, the Red Handler and the thief. The detective's stomach gave a rumble. The day hadn't gone according to plan for either one of them.

THE RED HANDLER AND
THE MUSICAL BANDIT

CHAPTER I

It was raining. It rained more and more often now. The Red Handler sat in the Opel with his seat back and listened as Gould's later *Goldberg Variations* mingled with the raindrops on the roof as he regarded the life outside his windshield. People were rushing past on all sides, hunching underneath umbrellas and newspapers they put frantically over their heads, as if afraid they'd disintegrate if they got wet.[63] He thought of a film he'd once seen.[64]

An individual suddenly caught the Red Handler's attention.[65] The figure wore a suit and sunglasses and had neither an umbrella nor rainboots. The person was moving furtively through the crowd and seemed altogether unbothered by the copious amounts of rain. The Red Handler decided to keep an eye on this man for a few minutes. Something was quite clearly off about him.[66]

Before he knew it, the shady individual snuck around a corner and the Red Handler lost sight of him.[67]

The Red Handler sighed, opened the door reluctantly, and stepped out into the rain. He was sure to catch cold from this.

"Goddammit." He hurried toward the street corner, cursing this fellow who couldn't have just stayed put a little while longer. Having no umbrella, he drew the collar of his coat up tight around his neck and—[68]

The suspicious individual at the end of the street turned abruptly and looked right at the Red Handler. Right at him. Took off his sunglasses. Didn't say a word. Then he turned back around and took off running under the bridge toward the amusement park.

The Red Handler stormed after him, into the endless rain.[69]

CHAPTER 3

The man in the suit ran. He ran like hell toward the large Ferris wheel that gleamed before them hypnotically in the smoldering dusk. His tie was draped over one shoulder and his suit jacket flapped about him, revealing a revolver in his shoulder holster.[70] The Red Handler felt the water thrashing his face, but didn't let it faze him.[71] This was no time for that.[72] He was hot on the heels of the bandit, fighting his way between raffle booths and carousels, shoving aside kids wearing oilskins and big smiles.[73] Little did they know of life's brutality. For now.

Then he saw it. The man stopped suddenly in front of the Ferris wheel and spoke to a man and a woman there. The weapon came out.

The sound of gunfire set the gulls off flapping toward a murky sky that had never spared the least thought for the world below it.[74] The woman collapsed like a heavy bundle and lay motionless on the wet pavement.

The murderer leaped into a pod on the Ferris wheel and began his ascent.

CHAPTER 4

He had no choice. The Red Handler sprinted toward the Ferris wheel and got into the first pod that arrived. The city below him grew tiny. He could see all the way to the harbor, all the way out to the islands, as far as the point where the sea began. He thought he could make out his own house. A red house, in any case. And he could see the murderer with the smoking revolver in his hand. The murderer was on his way down.[75]

A moment later and the Red Handler was on his way down, too. But now, the murderer was on his way up.

This went on for a while. The Ferris wheel presented no small difficulty when it came to nabbing someone. The distance between their pods was simply too great. The two men stared coldly at one another each time they came to the same height. This was unsustainable. That much was certain.

On the other hand, riding a Ferris wheel was not altogether undiverting. It had been too long since he'd last ridden one. He felt a pleasant tingle in his belly during each descent. The murderer vanished up in the air. Then it was the Red Handler's turn. Up he went. The murderer sailed down past the corpse before being swept up again. The Red Handler kept his eyes on him on the way down. He reflected. Then he gave a start. Well now . . . it wasn't as if the murderer had anywhere to run.

The Red Handler leaned back and let the wind tousle his hair. For a moment he forgot the current drama and imagined he was back in North Jutland, among the huts on Løkken Beach. What a wonderful summer that had been. And fall. Up till just before Christmas. Happy times. He'd lingered there too long. Far too long. But who could blame him?[76]

CHAPTER 5

He came to his senses again. Back to stone-cold reality. He was on his way down.

"Stop the wheel!" shouted the Red Handler as he began his climb. Dammit! There was his house again. Maybe.

"Stop the wheel, carny!" he shouted again when he reached the bottom. The unkempt Eastern European man, clearly the descendant of a long line of carnies, did promptly as he was told and the Ferris wheel ground to a halt.[77] Both men's journeys had come to an end.

CHAPTER 6

The Red Handler climbed carefully out of his pod and ordered the murderer lowered. A short time later and the two men stood face to face. The Red Handler forced him to look upon his deed.

"Now, what do you have to say about this?"[78]

The murderer said nothing.

"I said: What do you have to say about this?"

Still nothing. The murderer just looked at him.

"Do you have *anything* to say about this?" The Red Handler was beginning to feel a bit irritated.

Slowly, extraordinarily slowly, the murderer lifted his hands to remove the earbuds from his ears. The Red Handler hadn't noticed the black cords against the smart black suit.[79]

"Excuse me," said the murderer, "did you say something? I'm listening to the *Goldberg Variations*, you see."

The Red Handler was dumbfounded. That didn't happen very often. Now it was happening: He was dumbfounded.

"I asked you, what do you have . . . the *Goldberg Variations*, did you say?"

The murderer nodded as a grin took shape at the corners of his mouth.

"I see, but . . . Glenn Gould?"

"Who else?"

"The . . . short . . . or the long version?"

The murderer rolled his eyes in resignation.

"The short version, without all the lingering."[80]

For one second it was as if the Red Handler saw himself in the bandit. Another version of himself.

"I also prefer to play it that way," the murderer continued. "I am a concert pianist."

The Red Handler lit a cigarette.

"Not anymore, pal. Soon you'll be no more than a number and a prison uniform. What do you have to say in your defense?" The Red Handler purposely let a smoke ring rise slowly above the corpse.[81]

"That's my wife."

"You mean, that *was* your wife?"

The murderer burst into tears.

"My god, you're right. What have I done?"

"You've played your last danse macabre for a long time."

"I . . . I just got so jealous," the killer sobbed. "Of him!"

The Red Handler looked at the young fellow standing mournfully beside the dead woman. Then he looked back at the murderer. He nodded in a way that could have been perceived as sympathetic.[82]

"I see," the Red Handler said calmly. "I see."

CHAPTER 7

The old Opel darted through the evening streets on its way toward the jail. The amusement park grew smaller and smaller behind them. Neither of the men spoke, and as for the Red Handler, he had other things on his mind.

As soon as it was summer, he would go back to the beaches of Denmark.[83]

THE RED HANDLER AND
THE SECRET MASSAGE STUDIO

The night was bitter cold. The darkness clung to everything and everyone.[84] A thief lurked his way among the houses, on the way to his next victim, Dr. Kneipp.[85] Little did he suspect that the Red Handler too was on the prowl.

CHAPTER 2

Just as the thief was prying open the south window of the doctor's house, the Red Handler leaped forth like a gazelle, braced himself on an edge, and snatched the crook by the back of the neck.[86]

"Now I've got you!"

The thief sneered: "But I haven't done anything yet. You've got nothing on me."

The Red Handler fumed, but the lousy thief was right.

"Alright then. I'll just wait right here."

That was the Red Handler for you: always a step ahead. He smoked a menthol cigarette while the thief went to work.

Some minutes passed before the thief appeared in the window with his loot in a sack. The Red Handler laughed.

"Are you ready to head down to the slammer now?"

"Dammit," exclaimed the thief, "you are too good."[87]

The Red Handler ground out the cigarette with his toe.

"I know."

Together they walked the long way to the police station. Neither of them said a word about the massage studio.[88] The city was safe once more, if only for tonight.

THE RED HANDLER AND
THE LUCKY MURDERER

CHAPTER I

A deafening noise tore the night asunder.

The Red Handler's coffee mug fell to the floor by the window of his apartment, where he sat and observed the city's lost souls outside, as he often did when he couldn't sleep.[89] This was a big problem for him, all right. His parents had forced him to play the violin, and the blows the young Red Handler's fingers had endured from his teacher Gregorius's cane at every false note when he played the demanding *Goldberg Variations* had often caused his grip to fail him if he heard a sudden unfamiliar noise while concentrating.[90] Twelve years of therapy had done little except stoke his embittering bitterness. The lower part of one pants leg was soaked with the scalding liquid. It hurt and would leave a mark. But he had learned that crying was forbidden.[91] He turned in the direction of the sound and saw a young woman fall in the river with a splash.[92]

CHAPTER 2

The triggerman still held the smoking pistol in his hand.[93]

CHAPTER 3

"Hey, you!" shouted the Red Handler.

"Dammit!" the triggerman muttered and took off.

After a short, intense chase, the Red Handler laid the trig-german smack on the ground.[94]

"You'd better pray to God that girl isn't dead, since that would make you a murderer, and murderers go to jail, where they spend years behind bars. You'll be an old geezer before you draw another free breath."

"Oh, my. I hope I didn't kill her, then. Let's go down to the river and see what happened to her."[95]

They jogged down to the river.[96] The girl had crawled up onto the grass. She was bleeding from a wound on her right arm, but was in relatively good shape otherwise.

"It's all right," said the girl. "Only I must have struck a branch in the water down there. No way anyone could see it, really. Take the good luck with the bad, I guess. I wasn't shot, just so you know. He must have missed."[97]

The Red Handler looked sternly at the triggerman.

"You got lucky this time, but don't you imagine you're getting off scot-free. You have to face consequences, no matter how the cookie crumbles."

"I really didn't see that coming. But you're probably right." The triggerman put out his hands so the Red Handler could slap the cuffs on.

"I didn't bring my handcuffs, so all I can do is count on you not to cause more trouble. Can I?"

The triggerman nodded remorsefully.

"And one more thing . . ." said the Red Handler.

"What?"

"You owe me a coffee!"

They laughed.[98]

The young girl laughed too, but she was clearly in a lot of pain, so the laughter seemed a bit put on.[99]

In any case, she was alive. And that was a great deal more than you could say for most people.[100]

THE RED HANDLER AND THE TRAVELING SALESMAN WHO DIDN'T WORK FOR MICROSOFT

CHAPTER I

Night had fallen.[101] The Red Handler took his hands out of the hot-dog water just as he heard the doorbell ring. He studied his fingers briefly. They looked good. Elegant, almost.[102] Hard to believe, after so much wasted money on all the manicures, all the liters of lotions and creams, that a chance discovery would bring the long-sought miracle cure: lukewarm hot-dog water.[103] That is, if you could accept the occasional disadvantage of an unbalanced diet. He could have made a fortune by now, he thought while drying his hands with a dishcloth. Hot-dog water with a pinch of salt: his own patented formula. But no. He cared nothing for money.[104] He cared only for justice.

CHAPTER 2

The doorbell rang again. The Red Handler had been so occupied by the hot-dog water that he'd forgotten to open the door. Now he did so. It went well. He was good at opening doors, even though he disliked doing so. Bravo, Red Handler.[105] That was the word he used. "Bravo," he said once more. That was enough.

The figure at the door scowled at the inwardly rejoicing detective.

"Well, what is this about?" asked the Red Handler.

The figure pointed to an ID card on his chest.

"I'm from the alarm company," he said.

"Sector Alarm?"

"Let's not get hung up on details," answered the person while striding into the dimly lit apartment. "How many smoke alarms do you have?"

"I'm sorry, I don't let travelling salesmen inside."

"I'm not a travelling salesman."[106]

"And yet you're trying to sell me smoke alarms?"

"I'm only here to ask whether you are concerned for the safety of yourself and your family."

"I live alone."

"But, aren't you . . . expecting a little one? No?" said the salesman, nodding at the Red Handler's belly.[107]

"I'm on a hot-dog diet, and it's none of your business."

"I see. So you're spending lots of time in the kitchen. Huh. How many smoke alarms did you have, again?"

"One, I think."[108]

"Just one?" The salesman walked around the apartment and jotted a few notes. He left his shoes on. That was unacceptable. Absolutely unacceptable. But the Red Handler kept his mouth shut.

"Perhaps you don't care whether the entire place goes up in flames and with it all your memories and possessions. A few smoke alarms wouldn't be such a bad idea, no?"

"I'm afraid this isn't a good time," said the Red Handler. "I was just about to take a shower." This was true. He liked to bathe in the evenings to cleanse himself of the stench of lawlessness from the foregoing day and prepare himself to rein in the night's misdeeds. And anyway, why would he lie about that? Who in their right mind would lie about their bathing routine?[109]

"I see," said the salesman. "I can come back in a couple hours, if that would be better."[110]

"I do not wish to purchase any smoke alarms."

"I'm not trying to push you into anything. I just need to know how many you want to buy."

"No, thank you."

"But, what about the little one?"

"I am not pregnant."[111]

"You said that. But things happen. Things happen all the time. To anyone."

"This really is a bad time, I'm afraid . . ."

"I can come back. What time works for you?"

The Red Handler stared at the salesman. Long and hard.

"No, thank you. But what if I came to your home one evening when you're not at work?"

69

The salesman grinned. He was familiar with this ploy, this attempt at an insult. He'd been on the job for six months; he'd heard them all by now.

"Sure, why not," the salesman replied coldly.

The Red Handler detected the sarcasm, but had a comeback ready.

"Great. When is a bad time for you?"

"Next Wednesday at quarter to midnight? That would be an exceptionally bad time."

"Wonderful. I'm looking forward to it."

"Wonderful," answered the salesman with an idiotic smile. He should have known better.[112]

CHAPTER 3

At exactly 11:32 P.M. the Red Handler parked his car outside the salesman's house. He sat in his car for a few velvety
minutes to savor the end of the *Goldberg Variations*, the early
version this time, by a young, impatient Glenn Gould. It was
quite unsurpassed. Then he stepped out of his car, pulled tight
his trenchcoat, walked toward the house, and rang the doorbell. He thought he detected the odor of hot-dog water waft-
ing from under the front door. This made him feel anxious and
stressed. Then the salesman opened the door. The air was just a
bit musty.[113] The Red Handler let out a sigh of relief.

"What the hell are you doing here?" cried the salesman. "Do
you know what time it is? Have you lost your mind?"[114]

"Is this a bad time?"

"Jesus Christ, what an understatement!"

"Good."[115]

The Red Handler forced his way inside and entered the living room. The living room was dark but for the light from a
computer monitor. A handsfree headset lay on the table. Next to
it was a cassette deck playing the sound of office noise.

Hello? Are you there?

The voice came from the headphones. The Red Handler lifted the handsfree headset.

OK, I think I've done it right this time . . . are you able to log into my device now? The voice sounded on the verge of tears. *Oh my God, I'm so glad you called. Just think—to get a call from Microsoft Tech Support that my computer has a major security flaw! No wonder you're such a successful multinational corporation. Thank God help is on the way!*

The Red Handler glared hard at the salesman.

"You don't work for Microsoft, do you? And this guy doesn't have any problems with his computer, does he?"

The salesman trembled. "Cripes."

"How many people have you managed to scam? How much money have you stolen from them?"

The salesman, who did not work for Microsoft, hesitated.

"I don't know . . ."

"Out with it!"

"I . . . I'd have to check my Excel spreadsheet, and then . . ."

"Fine. Just print it out and we'll discuss it on the way to the slammer.[116] And print double-sided. You won't be including trees among your innocent victims."[117]

The salesman, not from Microsoft, realized the jig was up. He'd met his match.

"Dammit," he said quietly. "You caught me red-handed. You are too good."[118]

The Red Handler laughed quietly.

"Just doing my job."

He said it again. "Just doing my job."

Twice was enough.[119]

THE RED HANDLER AND
THE UNSOLVABLE MYSTERY OF
THE BURMESE CAT

CHAPTER I

The private detective looked with pride at the front door, where a brass plate shone with black lettering. THE RED HANDLER, PRIVATE DETECTIVE, it read.[120] Previously it had read only, THE RED HANDLERER, with a misspelling to boot thanks to the engraver's mix-up, but it too had been a custom-made brass plate. Before that, many years ago now, there had just been a torn sheet of paper with *The Red Handler* on it.[121] But he was a private detective now. No doubt about it. One only had to glance at all his exploits.[122] He glanced at them now, at the newspaper clippings covering the wall.[123] "The Master Detective!"[124] "Aplomb Itself!" "The Redoubtable Red Handler!" "Red Handler Gives Glimmer Man A Red Face!" "Red Handler To Bad Guys: I'll Handle You!" "Gotta Hand It To The Red Handler!" A lot of them contained puns and wordplay. That was the press for you. Had to make money somehow.[125]

There were more headlines than that. Many more. A couple of them even had the imprint of red lipstick from an old flame who'd been unable to restrain herself back then, but now no longer lay claim to the steamy love-stamp, even if she probably still swore by the same brand of lipstick.[126] He felt a certain urge to read all the press clippings. Perhaps even mimeograph some of them, make a nice little collage; get the Christmas presents done early this year.[127]

But there was no end to the work of a private detective, and no time to lose.

CHAPTER 2

He hunched over against the wind as he found his rhythm in the frigid evening. The streets were agreeably deserted, as people probably get ready in front of the mirror for another night on the town, sure to regret their drunken antics the morning after. That, or there was something good on TV, and no one had told him.[128]

CHAPTER 3

The Red Handler listened to the echo of his footsteps while he walked down the narrow cobblestone streets.[129] He had almost come to the streetcorner where, more often than not, one encountered sleaze that needed straightening out, when he heard the meowing of a cat close by. A plaintive, almost despairing wail.

With utmost care the Red Handler took a few steps into the near-darkness of the alleyway. He looked around. Nothing. Only two trash bins, along with a half-eaten kebab on the ground, or maybe a pigeon, it was hard to tell. But the sound did not let up. The cat continued to yowl somewhere close by. Had it damaged its paw? Did it have a tummyache?[130]

"Ps ps ps," he whispered. Listened.

The cat kept meowing in despair, clawed at the door.

The door.

He understood now. The cat was shut inside. The Red Handler slowly inspected the building's wooden exterior for a solution; once his eyes got used to the dark, he saw it.[131] A tiny door, right next to the ground, perhaps only 15 inches tall, but a door all the same. With a TrioVing lock and everything.[132] A strange affair. Almost as strange as the time he'd dreamed about a badger with AIDS and a top hat. But he'd been on a heavy regimen of penicillin at the time.[133]

He gingerly took hold of the doorhandle and turned it. The door was unlocked. He opened it.

A strange odor wafted out of the dark doorway. Then it appeared, the cat. It slipped outside and rubbed against the detective's corduroys. A little Burmese cat. Carefully, the Red Handler bent down and picked it up.

The cat weighed a ton.[134] He unwittingly dropped the animal. The Burmese cat landed on its feet, hissed at the Red Handler, and darted off into the alleyway and vanished. He stood there looking after it.

"You shouldn't have done that," said a voice.

The Red Handler spun around and saw a silhouette at the entrance to the alley that was illuminated by the streetlamps behind him.

"You shouldn't let cats roam free in this town," continued the man.

"Oh? And why is that?" asked the Red Handler, taking a step closer to the figure. He was unafraid. He was used to asking difficult questions.

"Because some cats have baggage," said the figure before taking off, out into the light and away.

The Red Handler remained standing alone. This was turning into one of those evenings. He wished he was at home with his newspaper collage right about now.

For several minutes more he stood there, turning the situation over in his mind.

Hmm.

Hmm.

Hmm.[135]

He made up his mind.

Screw it. Home to the collage. It was just too tempting.

CHAPTER 4

With a sophisticated wave of the hand he hailed a taxi.[136] He sat in the backseat and watched as the gloomy, dark city slid by outside the car window.[137] One part of him felt guilty for not staying out to fight for justice and public safety. Another part of him was thinking how nice it would be to sit down with the collage and some *Goldberg Variations*.[138]

It was then he saw it: the house along the street in which a light shone in one window.[139] A suspicious man stood halfway hidden behind curtains he couldn't possibly have picked out himself.[140] That was all the evidence he needed: somebody was up to shenanigans. There would be no collaging tonight, after all. The Christmas presents would have to wait.[141]

The Red Handler told the driver to stop, paid, got the receipt and put it in his wallet's compartment for tax-deductible travel expenses before storming up to the house, flinging open the door, and running up the stairs and into the room where the suspicious man stood looking at an enormous metal box.[142]

The private detective jabbed an accusing finger into the man's chest.[143]

"You! Out with it! What have you done? Where is your wife? Have you killed her?"

"How do you know I'm married?"

"Your curtains betrayed you. No man would have chosen that pattern by himself."

"Hmm . . . you are too good . . . too good."

"Thank you."

"And yet . . . what if I'd just gotten a divorce and hadn't had a chance to get new curtains?"

"But I'll bet you aren't divorced, are you?"

"Damn. You got me there, for sure."[144]

The Red Handler cast his eagle eye around the room.

"So where is the body? Where is your wife? And what the hell is this metal box?"

The man nodded to himself.

"That is the question, isn't it? Whether or not I killed my wife, I mean. I'm a scientist, you see. Quantum physics. I know a thing or two about this world and all that surrounds it."

"So do I, you better believe."[145]

"But not about this."[146]

"So, your wife is . . . inside the box?" the Red Handler asked almost in disbelief as he approached the object and began to loosen the chain the man had used to secure the lid.

"If you open the lid," said the man calmly, but firmly, "my wife, Beata, will either be dead or alive. That is beyond doubt. One or the other. But . . . if she's alive, you won't be able to arrest me, and if she's dead, that'll be on you, given that—relative to her quantum superposition—my wife is both alive and dead, and therefore neither-nor, or rather both-and, and as you well know, there are no laws that explicitly forbid the simultaneous murder and nonmurder of one's wife, to say nothing of asking her to climb into a metal box in order to nonmurder her. All in the name of, hehe, science. At the same time, you are now in the unenviable position of either not opening the metal box, which would make you a nondetective for failing to investigate the case, or opening it, which would either lead to my exoneration and loss of face for you, or else make you the catalyst of what is in theory my exclusively potential act of nonmurder, and you would thereby transcend yourself to become . . . the homicidal mastermind Red Handler."[147]

The Red Handler rubbed his moustache. "This is quite the pickle, if I do say so myself," he said.

"Well, what'll it be?"[148]

"Heh. You tell me."

He'd never said anything like this before. Perhaps a "heh," if only rarely, but never a "you tell me." Not in a million years.

"Well?" The potential murderer was growing impatient and nervous.

The Red Handler looked at his hands. Hmm. Never had he had felt such intense longing for a restful evening at home with a bowl of hot-dog water.

"I think," said the Red Handler, straightening himself up a bit, "I'll take the metal box home to examine it a while."

"But . . ." said the man.

"No buts about it."

"But, I . . . what does that mean? For me, that is?"

In one lightning-quick motion the Red Handler bust out his handcuffs and slapped them onto one of the man's wrists.

"It means you're under arrest for the murder of your wife, and simultaneously not under arrest."[149]

"But, I . . ." The man threw out his arms in despair. "What am I supposed to . . . This isn't fair! How am I to plan the next few days if I'm both going and not going to jail? I usually buy groceries a week at a time. What if they go bad before I've had a chance to eat them?"

"You should've thought about that before. Now you'll have to both go and not go to the store, eat and not eat dinner, while your wife is both dead and alive. Et cetera, as they say."

"My God . . . eternal uncertainty. The worst punishment of all! You truly are too good for your own good, Red Handler."[150]

The Red Handler turned to leave, but stopped.

He smiled, faintly.

CHAPTER 6

Back home he dipped his hands into the hot-dog water and sighed. What a day it had been. And not been.[151] Slowly, he turned and looked at the large metal box where the woman was stone dead but also alive and kicking, maybe even a tad impatient. He had a splitting headache. The floor was marred with deep grooves where he had pushed the box across the living room. The landlord sure wouldn't be thrilled. He ought to have put a blanket under the box, or at least some felt furniture pads; but it was too late to think about that now. He thought about something else entirely, but dared not say it loudly. He said it softly instead.

"This case is not yet solved."[152]

For the first time in as long as he could remember, the nauseating feeling crept in. Uncertainty. Doubt.[153]

THE RED HANDLER AND
THE DIFFICULT SABBATH

April. It was snowing. This was an unpredictable country. The Red Handler sat by his window regarding the streets as they grew whiter and whiter with each passing minute. The *Goldberg Variations*[154] flowed from the speakers on the secretaire. A cat, whose hind legs appeared to have been run over, dragged itself down the sidewalk. Long, glistening viscera or tapeworms protruded from the rectum.[155] The Red Handler looked within himself to see whether he felt any pity for the animal.[156] The past year had been tough, tougher than usual. And things were always tough, as a rule. After the incident with the Burmese cat and the paradoxical nonmurder, he felt something had come to a head.[157] For the first time in his life, he had sought refuge in religion and entered into what he would later call "my time of wandering." For one who had never once doubted or sought the aid of a higher power, he had become a shadow of his former self. This made his work easier, as far as it went, since as a shadow he could move unseen through the city's alleyways and streets, but he also felt far weaker than he had in a long time. He looked out the window again. The cat was gone. It could be dead now, for all he knew. A half hour later the phone rang. He answered it reluctantly.

A dark voice said: "Psst. Rumor has it that an armored car heist is taking place today, by the bridge." It grew silent a few seconds, as if the person on the other end was waiting until he was alone again. Then he continued: "At 4:15 exactly. By the bridge. Be there."

"Who is this?"

"None of your concern," said the voice and hung up.[158]

The Red Handler looked up at the clock. Ten minutes to noon. This was going to be a problem.

CHAPTER 2

He parked his Opel outside the brick building, walked slowly up the steps to the large, heavy wooden door, opened it, and slipped inside.

The anteroom was quiet, except for the hum of the AC unit and the heavy breathing of the secretary.

"I need to speak to the rabbi," the Red Handler said softly.

"Do you have an appointment?"

"No."

"The rabbi is a busy man."

"I know."

"It's Saturday."

"I'm aware."

She went back to her work as if that were the end of it. It wasn't. The Red Handler straightened himself and said again: "I really must speak with the rabbi."

"You said that."

"I did."

"This *is* Saturday."

"You said that."

"I did."[159]

They stared at each other a while. Another time, another place, who knew?[160]

"Let me check with him."

The secretary put down her papers, got up slowly and walked the long way toward the double doors of the rabbi's office and cautiously knocked. She walked in and closed the door behind her.

Shortly after she emerged again.

"The rabbi can see you now."

CHAPTER 3

Rabbi Chaim Mandelspritzer had been the Red Handler's confidant and adviser for close to a year now. He was a plump man in his 60s, of limitless wisdom and very limited time. The Red Handler sat down on the small chair in front of the huge desk and got straight to the point.

"There's going to be an armored car heist at 4:15 this afternoon," he said. "I can prevent it."

The rabbi nodded with understanding.

"It's Saturday," he said.

"I know."

"Saturday is the sabbath, my son."[161]

"That's just it. The question, I presume, is whether it would be *assur* to nab the thieves."

Rabbi Mandelspritzer leaned back heavily in the creaking leather chair.

"Oy, that's quite the dilemma."[162]

"That's why I came over as fast as I could."

"I appreciate that."

The rabbi scratched his head. For several moments. It was a big head.

"What do the scriptures say about Saturday work in these cases?" asked the Red Handler.

"Well, the Torah is not absolute when it comes to a case like this, according to the Talmud. God has a brain, but also a heart for those who suffer. Would anyone suffer by this . . . heist?"

"Yes, rabbi."

"I see. Well, let me see . . . Exodus, Chapter 34, verse 21 says: 'Six days thou shalt work, but on the seventh day thou shalt rest; in plowing time and in harvest thou shalt rest.' And Numbers, Chapter 15, verses 32–39 is fairly clear on the matter: 'And while the children of Israel were in the wilderness, they found a man gathering sticks upon the sabbath day. And they that found him gathering sticks brought him unto Moses and Aaron, and unto all the congregation. And they put him in ward, because it had not been declared what should be done to him. And the LORD said unto Moses: "The man shall surely be put to death; all the congregation shall stone him with stones without the camp." And all the congregation brought him without the camp, and stoned him with stones, and he died, as the LORD commanded Moses. And the LORD spoke unto Moses, saying: "Speak unto the children of Israel, and bid them that they make them throughout their generations fringes in the corners of their garments, and that they put with the fringe of each corner a thread of blue. And it shall be unto you for a fringe, that ye may look upon it, and remember all the commandments of the LORD, and do them; and that ye go not about after your own heart and your own eyes, after which ye use to go astray.'" Are you going about after your own heart and your own eyes, my son?"

"No."

"Good. Let us look at the matter more closely. The Mishnah, of course, lays out that we must not work the fields on a Saturday, nor tread the grapes, place loads on any beast of burden, buy or sell or otherwise engage in commerce, carry from one place to another, nor may we travel—let me ask you, how long is it from here to the bridge?"

"Half a mile, maybe. A mile, tops."

The Red Handler glanced up at the clock. It was already 2.

"Got it. Right . . . very walkable. So, to go on, we must not kindle a fire, sow, reap, plow, thresh, winnow, sift, gather into a pile, bake, knead, and so on; nor may we shear wool, whiten it, comb it, straighten it, dye it, spin it, stretch the threads of the warp in the loom, construct meshes, weave threads, sever threads, ravel or unravel, tie or untie knots, thread a needle, nor—"

"With all due respect, Rabbi Mandelspritzer, I—"

"One moment. One thing at a time. Where was I? Right, tying or untying, goes without saying . . . did I mention weaving already? I lost where I was. In any case, no weaving. Important. Also no sewing, ripping apart, writing upon or making sheepskin parchments, slaughtering, flaying, salting the hide, erasing—that is, erasing words you have written, not that that's allowed either. Writing, I mean. No using a highlighter (no matter what color, but I would imagine especially yellow and pink, they're the most common, but also blue, lots of people apparently go for blue nowadays. Oy vey.), to build, to dismantle, to carry—Did I say that already? But carrying anything, that is to say, from a private to a public place or a public to a private place and probably not within said public and/or private place either. In short, no carrying. But here, as elsewhere, we must not take scripture absolutely. Surely, some carrying must be done. The ambulance driver who couldn't get his shift moved, must be able to carry the injured from the wreckage. Look at it that way. You can think of any number of examples. In the end, use your best judgement. And of course, one must never begin the final push on any job begun before the sabbath. The Mishnah also adds that one must never take on any activity that in form or content resembles any of the foregoing, for example, one must not tear a paper into small bits, since to do that would be like cutting paper, which for some is an honorable profession. And what of climbing trees, since the branches can break and that would be like trimming the bushes or chopping the tree down entirely. That sort of thing. And—"

"I'd just like to—"

It was 3 o'clock. Just over an hour before the heist.

"Don't interrupt. Let's see . . . ah, yes, nor is it permitted to water flowers or make a bouquet. What else? Did I mention the thing about no weaving? Good. To separate fresh from rotten fruit, brush or wash or wipe dirt off of shoes and clothes, cut hair, trim nails, apply makeup: forbidden, forbidden, forbidden, all of it. Taking blood samples: also forbidden. Face lotion, shampoo, and other assorted personal hygiene products: forbidden. And . . . one may not sharpen pencils, paint, draw, open umbrellas or otherwise engage in any other form of sun protection, not that that's a big worry today, what with all this snow, and yet, and yet, forbidden, nonetheless. Having a smoke? Using your phone? Nuh-uh. Turning the lights on and off? Forget it. And while you're at it, no winding your grandfather clocks or setting your watches. Any use of glasses beyond what is strictly necessary: that's a no-no. And then there all the things that are *muktzeh* and may not be touched: money, personal checks, scissors, hammers, pencils and pens, battery-powered toys and flashlights, compact discs, telephones and computers, not to mention religious objects like the shofar, tefillin, and lulav. Hands off. Look at it that way. The shabbat candles, too, are *muktzeh*. Oh, and no packing suitcases, I almost forgot. No rearranging furniture, opening mail, discussing cash flows or anything else having to do with money or for that matter anything having to do with

94

daily life at all. Also forbidden to think about the week ahead. And, well, it goes on in that key."[163]

"So, what do you think? What would you advise me to do in this case?"

The rabbi drummed his fingers on the table and looked out the window a few seconds. The clock had passed 4.

"I really don't see why you couldn't stop that cargo from being stolen."

"Thank you."

"But maybe see to it you're back before sundown."[164]

CHAPTER 4

He looked up at the clock. Damn. He was already late. The Red Handler sped away in his old Opel and arrived just in time to see a black SUV swerve in front of the armored car in the middle of the bridge, effectively stopping it.[165] From his car he could spy the rotten scoundrel firing his machine gun toward his target. An infernal noise was heard all over the town as bullets ricocheted off the back doors of the armored car. Cars were skidding to a halt on either side of the bridge. Screams from young and old alike filled the air.[166]

The Red Handler leaped from the vehicle and tore off toward the robber, who was too busy plundering to notice the detective charging after him.[167] With enormous power the Red Handler dove toward the robber's feet at the last second, knocking him over. The weapon flew out of his hands, turning a few somersaults in the air before vanishing over the railing and into the water a hundred meters below. The armored car driver climbed out of the cabin; fortunately, he was unharmed.

"Thank God you've come!" he exclaimed with a trembling voice as onlookers approached to console him.

If only you knew how right you are, thought the Red Handler. But he didn't say it. He was too busy slapping the handcuffs on the baby-faced perpetrator.[168]

"Off to jail with you, mister," said the Red Handler icily. "You'll have more than enough time to think about what you have done. *A broch tzu day lebn!*"[169]

The reckless criminal made no answer, but stayed totally calm. To the Red Handler it looked as if he were weeping.

"Are you weeping? Well, that serves you right. It's only right you'd feel sorry for what you've done. Today is the sabbath. A day for rest and contemplation. And this is anything but kosher."

"I . . . I am so sorry," the young robber sobbed. He couldn't have been a day older than 18. "This is my first hold-up. I've never done anything like this, I swear."

"Your criminal bar mitzvah, in other words."

"I don't want to be a crook."

The Red Handler nodded meaningfully. "There, there. Some people are like this and others are like that and that's just how it is." He pulled the hoodlum up to his feet and pushed him toward the Opel as the onlookers applauded. But just as the assailant was about to be pushed into the backseat, he suddenly protested.

"I won't, I won't! I'm scared!"

"Scared of what?"

"Of . . . prison. And the kinds of things that, you know, go on in there . . ."

"Oh, it's really not as bad as all that. Why, I'll just give you some *Tex Willer* comics and it'll fly by."[170]

"Thank you."

"No problem. We'll stop at my place on the way to the station and pick up a whole stack of them for you to read in the slammer."

"You're too kind."

"That is in the eye of the beholder. Always. Always the eye of the beholder. Never forget that."

CHAPTER 5

It was morning the next day by the time he finally made his way back home; he hadn't been able to finish by sundown. Now the sun was on its way back up again. The Red Handler drove around his block a couple times, looking for a parking space. Finally he found one on a side street. He started walking the rest of the way home, deep in his own thoughts, when a man called out to him.

"Excuse me?"

The Red Handler turned toward the sound. A man dressed in white stood in the doorway of the bakery on the other side of the street. The bakery was full of activity inside, probably had been all night. People would never lose their taste for fresh bread on a Sunday morning. The Red Handler crossed the street and walked toward the baker, who stood with his hand outstretched.

"Bun?"

The Red Handler nodded.

The baker raised the bun, split it in two, and handed one piece to the Red Handler.

They ate without a word, but both had the same thought: the Red Handler had failed as a Jew. Now, he was only the Red Handler again.

But at least the snow had stopped.[171]

THE RED HANDLER ON VACATION
IN DENMARK

CHAPTER I

No one could deny he deserved a trip in Denmark now. After everything that had happened. Copenhagen . . . sweet Jesus, what a town! He loved it there, especially the seedy area around Isted Street.[172] The night before, he'd hardly been able to sleep, he was so on edge about whether he'd get to see her again. But finally he did sleep. Some time later, he woke up.[173]

CHAPTER 2

The Red Handler drank a glass of brewer's yeast and brushed his teeth that morning before jogging down to the train station and finding the right platform.[174] He settled into the carriage, stretched out his legs, and looked forward to the long train ride. Then, he arrived at his destination.

CHAPTER 3

It was raining in Denmark. He'd forgotten his umbrella at home. *Fuck*, he said to himself. He was wet, and that might mean catching cold. Everything would be ruined.

CHAPTER 4

As the rain beat down upon his hat, he spotted a mysterious figure sneak into one of the train station's back doors.[175] Without hesitating the Red Handler tore off after the figure, into the building, up the stairs, down through long, desolate corridors, and into the innermost room in which the mysterious figure was bent over what could only be described as: a bloody corpse.[176]

The corpse was dead.[177] The Red Handler didn't even need to check for a pulse to confirm it. His own pulse was pounding furiously: He was in Denmark.[178] That's how it was in this country. Raw and brutal. He might not get time to kiss his old flame after all.[179]

The Red Handler sucked a mint pastille slowly and pointed at the mysterious figure, whose back was still turned, and who bent over the corpse with a smoking gun in one hand.[180]

"Are you the one who did this?"

"What are you talking about?" the mysterious figure protested.

"Are you the killer?"

The mysterious figure turned toward the Red Handler and threw out his arms in resignation.

"Damn, you caught me hook, line, and sinker. But tell me: How did you get wise to me?"[181]

"Your fatal mistake was when you decided to look mysterious."[182]

"Well, I'll be . . . But there's no sense denying it. You're good. Too good. I guess I'm in for a long jail sentence now."

The Red Handler nodded gravely. "That sounds about right. You're coming with me to the police station to face the consequences of what you have done."

The killer stared at the floor, chastened.[183]

"Who are you?" he asked.

"I'm the Red Handler," answered the Red Handler.

"Now, that's appropriate," said the killer.

CHAPTER 7

Outside, the rain had stopped and the sun had come out. But in so many ways, it was still dark out.[184]

THE RED HANDLER AND
THE PRESUMPTUOUS MURDERER

CHAPTER I

It was morning. He wasn't wearing clothes.[185] The doorbell rang. He hated it when the doorbell rang. That's why he no longer rang doorbells himself.[186] Not unless he had to. Not unless it was, as they say, strictly necessary. As was probably the case now. Someone had the need to do this or that. And that is why the doorbell rang.[187]

It rang again. He decided to open the door if it rang a third time.

He opened the door.[188] And he stood face to face with a man who looked just like him, dressed in his own clothes.

"What are you doing here?" asked the man.

The Red Handler felt confused. That wasn't a good feeling. It reminded him of an episode with his aunt when he was five.[189]

"I live here," answered the Red Handler.

"No," said the person calmly. "I live here. What is your name?"

"The Red Handler," said the Red Handler. "And you?"

"The Red Handler," said the person who was obviously not the Red Handler, since one of the few certainties the Red Handler had had up to this point, was that he was the Red Handler, and so the person who stood here claiming to be the Red Handler, could not be the Red Handler.[190] The situation was delicate. And, as noted, confusing. "I think you'd better let me in so we can clear this up."

The Red Handler decided to play along. He let the man in.

CHAPTER 2

The man who claimed to be the Red Handler walked straight to the closet, took out the suitcase the Red Handler always used on his trips to Copenhagen, and began filling it with clothes.

"What . . . are you doing?" the Red Handler asked the not-Red Handler.[191]

"I'm going away for a bit. Please do not disturb me while I'm packing."

The situation was tense. The man clearly knew where his (the Red Handler's) things were.

The Red Handler scratched his leg. The old bullet wound was starting to act up.[192] He ought to have put on some pants, a shirt at least. But something told him that this was no time for trifles.

The not-Red Handler closed the suitcase with a bang and walked briskly toward him. He raised a threatening finger to the Red Handler's face.

"Have you seen my Glenn Gould record?"

"But . . ."

"No buts. Where is it?"

The Red Handler knew exactly where it was. But was it wise to say it? Shouldn't he keep quiet? He said it.[193]

113

"On the shelf behind you," he said.

"I thought so," said the not-Red Handler. "I'd also like back my wallet and the keys to the Opel."

CHAPTER 3

The two Red Handlers sat each in a chair staring intensely at one another while Gould's piano music transpired from the speakers, as did time. They looked at the clock in silence. The train to Copenhagen left in an hour, and only one of them would be on board.[194] The consequences could be catastrophic. At the same time, the Red Handler felt a twinge of uncertainty in the back of his neck. What if this man was right? What if he wasn't the Red Handler? What if he ... he didn't even want to think about it.

Just then, the telephone rang.[195]

The Red Handler didn't like to talk on the telephone, either.[196]

But now it was ringing.[197]

One of them had to answer it.[198]

They looked at each other.[199]

They looked at the telephone.[200]

Back at each other.[201]

At the telephone.[202]

At each other.[203]

At the telephone, again.[204]

And then back at each other.[205]

It stopped ringing.[206]

"We missed the call," said the not-Red Handler calmly, nodding at the telephone.

The Red Handler sucked at his teeth and studied the man who might be him.

"They'll call back if it's important," he said, adding, "They always do."

The next second, it rang again.[207] The Red Handler reached out and picked up the receiver before the other got the chance.[208]

"Hello?"

"Is this the Red Handler?" asked a mysterious voice.[209]

"What is this about?"

"Is anyone else there now?"

"Yes."

"Don't let him leave. Whatever you do: don't let him leave. We have . . ."

"Who's 'we'?"[210]

"That's not important right now. Okay? I'm calling about a murderer who is pretending to be you in order to hide his tracks. We have reason to believe that he . . ."

"That what?"

"That he has plans to hide you, too. You get me?"

"I sure do."

The not-Red Handler leaned forward impatiently. "Who are you talking to?"

"My aunt," said the Red Handler while listening to the voice on the other end.[211]

"My aunt? Tell her I'll call back later. Once I'm in Copenhagen."[212]

The Red Handler hung up and stared right down the barrel of his own revolver. This was one hell of a pickle.

"Are you going to shoot me?"

"Why shouldn't I? I'm you, don't you see that? You're no longer . . . useful."[213]

116

CHAPTER 4

The two men remained seated in reverberant silence. One of them was not who the other one was. The clock on the wall ticked, each second marking the countdown of a life down to zero. The rising sun pierced through the open window, forming a halo around the Red Handler's head. A train to Copenhagen would soon be leaving. Only one of the two men loved that town. And there was only room for one of them on that train.[214]

Without warning a sharp sound tore through the room. *The doorbell rang.* Instinctively the not-Red Handler got up and ran to the entryway.

The Red Hander sat a moment or two, relieved, above all, before he stood up and used the opportunity to sneak into his bedroom to fetch his handcuffs.[215]

While digging through his nightstand drawer he heard voices out front. *Hi there, package from DHL, just sign here, please? One moment, please. Let's see. There, thank you.*

DHL. Holy God, that must be the new holster from Lawman Leather he'd been looking forward to so much that he'd barely slept all week.[216]

The Red Handler maneuvered without a sound into the entryway and lunged at the not-Red Handler with tremendous power. A scuffle ensued. Then it was over. The Red Handler caught a glimpse of the delivery man running away at the sound of the handcuffs clicking around the intruder's wrists. He lifted the scumbag to his feet.

"There'll be no Copenhagen for you today. It'll be four walls and a locked door."

The not-Red Handler tried to wring free. He shouted. But it was useless. He crumpled to the floor.

"You are too good," he whispered. "Much too good . . ."

"You shouldn't have run to answer the door. I'd never have done that. Tell me, now, are you the one who . . ."

"Yes, I am the killer," hissed the man. "Don't push me any further, I can't take much more of this grilling, I just can't. It was I who killed those three women. I'll tell you everything."[217]

"The only thing I want to know now is how you know so much about me. And who you are."

"Franz. My name is Franz," began the man, weeping. "I . . . I followed your career as carefully as I could, read everything about you, okay? All the write-ups, interviews. Also . . ."

"Yes?"

"Christ! I told you, don't push me. I . . . So, I've also been coming in at night while you're asleep. I learned every inch of your apartment, helped myself to your clothes, studied your routine, I . . . I admire you. In a way."[218]

"You can keep admiring me from a jail cell. You'll be sitting there until long after I'm gone."[219]

"I even knew about how you never answer the door at the first ring, but I . . . I just couldn't help myself! I . . ." The murderer struggled to get the words out. "When I was a kid, I only had one birthday party. Do you have any idea what it's like, getting to celebrate your birthday just one single time? Do you? Just so you know, it's . . . not good, okay? I'd been looking forward to it for months, Red Handler, to that day, the day that would be mine, mine alone, and then . . . and then they all came. My friends! The doorbell rang, and when I opened, a friend stood there. And then the doorbell rang again. And yet another friend stood there smiling with a present under their arm. Get the picture? The doorbell rang again and again and friend after friend kept coming into our home, into . . . happiness. A feeling I've never felt ever again. No one rings my doorbell anymore. So when I heard that sound, that glorious sound, I just . . . I just couldn't help myself."[220]

"That doesn't absolve you from what you've done. Not even a little bit."

The Red Handler raised the murderer to his feet again and told him to wait in the entryway until he'd put some clothes on.

"But know this, Red Handler!" said the murderer while the Red Handler was in the bedroom putting on pants, one leg at a time. "Know this: Everyone you arrest is yourself. And don't you forget it."[221]

But the Red Handler didn't hear him.

THE RED HANDLER AND THE
OUT-OF-CONTROL URINE

CHAPTER I

The Red Handler stood in a stall within the train station's public restroom and let it rip. Suddenly he heard someone clamor into the stall next to his. A male voice exclaimed: *aaahh!* A few seconds later, the Red Handler noticed something wet running toward his shoes. He recoiled, before quickly bending down and feeling the floor. It was wet all right.[222]

He rubbed it between his fingers. It was wet, without question. It looked like . . . piss. It smelled like piss, too.

And it tasted like piss.

God almighty.

CHAPTER 2

This will not do, thought the Red Handler.[223]

Quick as a leopard the Red Handler leaped onto the toilet and peered over the edge of the neighboring stall.[224] He pointed an accusing finger at the miscreant.

"Now I've caught you!" he roared.

The businessman was caught with his pants down, but had no intention of giving up so easily.

"It was an accident. Jesus Christ, man, chill."

"I don't believe in accidents, or chilling. You're coming with me where you belong: behind bars."

The businessman shook his head and pulled up his pants.

"Jesus, what's your problem?" he said wearily, throwing his arms out in disbelief. "It's just piss. Get some toilet paper and wipe it off."

"You can talk all you want, but you'll never talk your way out of this fix. Come out of there, and after we've both washed our hands, I'll handcuff you. In that order."

The miscreant/businessman gave a loud groan.

"Seriously, now you've lost it, Red Handler. Something's not right with you. Or is there now a law against reckless urination? Shouldn't you be going after real criminals, you know, murderers and thieves?"

It was the Red Handler's turn to scoff. He scoffed.[225]

"No crime is too small," he began. "If I looked the other way, everything would go to hell before you know it."[226]

"I. Didn't. Do. Anything. Wrong," protested the man in the stall next to him.

"Lies," said the Red Handler, poking a wet finger in the man's temple. "Because that's how it all starts. You start out with the petty stuff, and before you know it you're off murdering someone. I see it happen all the time. I've seen almost everything, if I may say so."

CHAPTER 4

And it was true. The Red Handler had seen a lot. Too much, according to many.

CHAPTER 5

The miscreant realized he had no chance.

"Fine. I'll take your word for it. Just let me go and wash my hands first."

"You better not try and use too-hot water," said the Red Handler. He was wise to all their tricks, these people. "I don't want you scalding yourself so you can accuse me of private-eye brutality."[227]

"I promise I won't."[228]

CHAPTER 6

The miscreant kept his word. He washed his hands at a moderate temperature, making sure to also wash in between the fingers, the back of each hand, and the fingertips, following the entire eight-point procedure for hand hygiene as outlined by the Norwegian Institute of Public Health. The Red Handler had to admit he was impressed. One could learn a thing or two by watching this man. But he slapped the handcuffs on the businessman all the same as soon as both were finished. He had no choice. There was a book, and it had to be followed. Consequences were inevitable.[229]

CHAPTER 7

The aroma of lavender wafted about the two figures as they slowly made their way to the police station.[230] The day was still young.

THE RED HANDLER COMES
TOO LATE

CHAPTER I

He was disappointed. It was a feeling he knew all too well.[231]
You might even say it constituted his basic attitude toward life.
There was hardly anything that hadn't disappointed him at one
point or another over the years. The weather, for instance. Almost always, the weather.[232] And the Christmas presents people
gave him from year to year; they'd never once failed to disap-
point. The last few years, he'd gone to Copenhagen instead of
seeing family.[233] Sat alone in a hotel. Drank. It had been okay.

What else? The amount of time milk was good for, of course. Disappointingly short. Someone ought to do something about that. Not to mention most of the shows on television, wave dampeners in waterbeds, the comfort of airplane seats, the long-term effects of acupuncture, instant coffee, the police work in this town, the court system, dinner parties, coq au vin, and tiramisu, nearly always served with a liberal sprinkling of disappointment right on top of the chocolate. The list was endless.[234] And people. Almost everyone he'd ever met, especially women, had all disappointed him in the end. Only Glenn Gould seemed to have kept his promise. But Glenn Gould was dead.[235]

CHAPTER 3

The latest offshoot from the towering tree of disappointment
was the film he'd sat and watched, a spy thriller of dubious quality and confusing plot. In the video store, upon finding what
appeared to be the only Clint Eastwood film he'd never seen,
he'd thought he'd hit the jackpot. It was only once he got home
and the amateurish opening scenes made him study the DVD
cover more closely, that he realized he'd read it wrong in his
excitement. The lead role was played by one Cliff Eastwood,
a totally unknown actor of Eastern European appearance who
spoke with a thick accent.[236] True, the film was praised by the
director Leslie Stevens and had won the Kvalito Premion prize
at an Esperanto film festival in the same country to which the
cast and crew belonged, but it was hard to know how strong the
competition had been.[237] [238] But having watched half of it already, he had to see how it ended. Plus, the woman who'd played
a bitter bar waitress in the film's first, unsteady minutes had a
certain captivating air of yearning about her. He hoped they'd
show her more as the film went on.

For some reason he started to feel impatient. Like an itch on
the back of his neck. He got up to fetch a ginger beer from the
refrigerator and glanced at his telephone.

Four missed calls, each within a few minutes of one another. All from the same number.

He took a swig and called back, as the mild beverage worked its way down his throat to settle in the lonesome darkness in the pit of his stomach, there to dwell with his anguish.

The voice that answered quickly sounded familiar. Probably Bernt. But you could never be too sure.

"I've been trying to reach you for an hour!"[239]

"I'm sorry, I ..." The Red Handler didn't like to admit it, but he too needed a break now and then, a break from everything. "I've been watching ... a movie."

The other end was silent.

"Which one?"

The Red Handler had to look at the box. In the initial glee at finding what he thought was a Clint Eastwood film, he hadn't even looked at the title.

"*Ŝancoj de doloro en la lando de murdo.*"

Silence again. The silence lingered in the air, forebodingly. Bernt, or whoever it was, sighed.

"Oh. Well, the woman is the killer."

"Are you sure?"

"Yes. Now you're needed elsewhere, Red Handler. Forty-two Orion Street. Now! Wait much longer, and the bodies'll start piling up in that house."

The person hung up. The Red Handler stood holding the telephone for a moment, hesitating. The recent episode in the train station restroom had done something to him, as if suddenly he no longer felt like doing anything, as if all he wanted was to sit in his chair and watch as the catastrophes piled up all around and buried him, whether the yearning bar waitress was the culprit or not.[240] It was as if he longed for the ultimate consequence of all things.[241]

136

It had grown late. Late on earth.[242]

But he got going. He had to. That was who he was. It was all he was.

CHAPTER 4

He sped through town, the houses flew past and became streaks of color, and time itself shattered in a million pieces as the Opel barreled through the sparse traffic and his impatient headlights lunged toward the address he'd gotten the tip about.[243]

Reality hit him smack in the face. The Red Handler saw it immediately when he turned onto the street: a body lay sprawled on the lawn outside the burning house, badly mangled. He parked the car and walked slowly over to it. What tragedy.

Out of routine, thoroughness, and an overwhelming despair, he scoured the whole area for the murderer. He found nothing. Not a goddamn fucking thing.[244]

Then the blue lights arrived. Sirens. Lights came on in the homes of curious neighbors. The Red Handler turned around and stood face to face with the police and the fire department.

It was then he realized: he had come too late.[245]

CHAPTER 5

He lay awake and heard footsteps in the stairway. A thud echoed through the walls when the postman flung the day's paper on the doormat. The Red Handler plodded through his apartment, opened the door, and stared at the boldface headline: "Arsonists Apprehended; Glimmer Man Saves Four, Whereabouts Now Unknown."[246]

He made coffee, read. A neighbor was quoted about the gunfire she'd heard, about the Glimmer Man's dramatic chase through the neighborhood, and how at last he singlehandedly ambushed the two killers without regard for his own safety.[247] She recounted in detail how the Glimmer Man had collapsed in the grass and wept over the one life he hadn't been able to save, while the killers writhed in handcuffs on the ground behind him. The Glimmer Man had lit incense for the deceased and said Kaddish, even though he was not in a minyan.[248] Then, he'd taken the killers with him and left. Without a word.[249]

CHAPTER 6

The sun sparkled outside. Inside him it was raining.[250]

The Red Handler got dressed, put the Eastwood film on the console in the entryway, and got ready to go return it, though he hadn't finished it.

Noch ist Polen nicht verloren, he thought.

But he didn't say it out loud.

THE RED HANDLER LANDS IN
TROUBLE WITH THE AUTHORITIES

CHAPTER I

The Red Handler sat still, and[251] [252]

I'm not here

This isn't happening

ENDNOTES

¹ My very first thought, when Frode Brandeggen showed up unannounced at my office in Dresden one afternoon in 2013 with the *Red Handler* manuscripts, was, in all its prosaic terseness, as follows: This is not particularly good. My subsequent thought, I imagine, was a corruption of the first, and went something like this: This is really, really not good. Dutifully—for I am nothing if not dutiful—I leafed through the heap of papers while he waited impatiently by the window, as I wondered why he'd come all this way to meet me, of all people. How had he even managed to find me? He told me about the one novel he'd had published, his subsequent jobs as a trash collector and library attendant, and the literary comeback he was preparing with what he called "a new form." I eventually asked him to step out for a while and come back toward dusk. Then I began reading. As I mentioned, this was more out of duty than anything else. I'm not an editor, I don't decide what and what not to publish, I only explain and add context to what others have accepted, what others deem important, canonical, consequential. No one ever asks me: *What do you think about this?* My sense of duty, therefore, was challenged by the humility I felt before this author, who said he knew my work as an annotator from a long line of scholarly editions now considered classic in Germany. He told

me he appreciated what he termed my "ability to read clearly." So read I did, in the hours he spent wandering Dresden. I read, I read again, and little by little, I was transformed. Since then, night has fallen, and everything has taken on significance. As afternoon turned to evening, above all it was Brandeggen's fury that stood out to me, the literary obstinance that would keep me returning to these texts time and again, the uncompromising tenor that emerges in spite of what seems, at first glance, to be the reductive language of crime fiction, the comic-strip sense of narrativity. This too is why—now that I've agreed to write endnotes to this first edition of Brandeggen's crime novels, ostensibly because he asked for it, in the papers he left to me—I have to treat Brandeggen's project with the utmost seriousness, even if that makes me his Sancho Panza. And it has been liberating, so very liberating for my work on this book, to dare, after so long, to step out of my accustomed shadows, to decide for myself the relevance of these endnotes to the text, to strike my own course and enter nothing but what I deem necessary. I should also add that the conversation that began that evening between me and Brandeggen would last three years. I don't believe he had many other people to talk to. But talk we did, by telephone, by letter, during my visits to him in Stavanger or, more often, in my welcoming him to Dresden, where he made do with the tiny guest room I'd fitted out in my apartment. Before him, I'd never had any guests. But if I may say so, I don't believe anyone knew Frode Brandeggen in his last days quite like I did. I say this not to lay claim to any role in his success, should these books move readers as much as they have moved me. I say this, rather, because of the way it foreshadows this man's terrible loneliness. The anger I find in these books is real, as is the despair that precipitated his dramatic swerve away from his avant-garde beginnings. It may be that that anger can only be grasped within the context of the gulf between his first book and the Red Handler. But the anger, nonetheless, doesn't give us the whole picture, because Brandeggen also cares all too much about his protagonist. His interest in the Red Handler, his level of concern and sympathy for his character, is genuine. As the author, his emotional stake is palpable, essential. The texts can never fully hide that they are fundamentally about Brandeggen himself, about a man who obviously is deeply troubled, and who, more than opposing crime literature *an sich* or the book industry's thirst for profit, is desperately trying to create a world with some semblance of meaning and predictability, where the structures are clear and there is such a thing as sincerity.

[2] When, eventually, Frode Brandeggen learned to accept the fate of his 2,322-page debut novel, *Conglomeratic Breath* (*Konglomeratisk pust*), ⁂ from then on forgoing the avant-garde in favor of chiseled-down, commercial crime fiction, he still held out some hope that the world might one day accommodate a more expansive, exploratory mode of literature. In the very first stages of the Red Handler project, Brandeggen wrote a separate novel as both a warm-up to the Red Handler universe and (he hoped) a standalone work in its own right. From what I have gleaned, he never mentioned this work to anyone. The unpublished novel, *All of These Loves* (*Alle disse kjærlighetene*, 433 pages in manuscript) deals with the Red Handler's relationship with his wife Gerd in Haugesund, where the Red Handler—who here seems to have a proper first and last name, though both are crossed out throughout the entire manuscript—works part-time as an electric meter reader. The novel is a passionate account of their intense love and often exemplary marriage that slowly but surely becomes counterproductive, to put it mildly, culminating in a magnificent scene in which the Red Handler persona is born and the

protagonist leaves Haugesund for good. There are hints toward the end of the manuscript that the wife leaves the Red Handler for his future nemesis, the Glimmer Man. There is no evidence Brandeggen was ever in a serious relationship himself.

⁂ From the back cover of *Conglomeratic Breath*: "*Imper Akselbladkvist is turning his house upside down in search of something he has lost. But is it really his house? And has he really lost anything? And if so, then what? Himself? Or everyone else? Distended and distracted by existential angst, he ambushes the constituent parts of his life (is it really his life?) through an intense, ruthless, and often heartrendingly intricate exploration of the potential Heidegger-plagiarist level of the self, represented by the distance between two threads of an almost fully disintegrated bedspread that his grandmother (if she is even his grandmother—and for that matter, how do we know she was really all that grand?) bequeathed him. Through more than two thousand pages— free from even the slightest scintilla of what Imper Aksel- bladkvist calls deformative abominations like punctuation and paragraph, chapters, and other readerly crutches—the author delves further and further into the bedspread, into the threads, into the yearning for his own constitutive fi- bers, and ultimately, his own text. That is—if we can even call it a text? And is it really a novel? And if it is, how can we know that the novel is his?*"

[3] Prior to my work on these endnotes, I read out of curiosity Brandeggen's debut novel, *Conglomeratic Breath*. Or, I should say, I tried. The publisher, Gyldendal, released the book back in 1992, but when I started asking around, no one could tell me anything about it. There were no reviews, no record of any

frode_brandeggen

konglomeratisk_pust
roman

Gyldendal Norsk Forlag

readings, no book festival appearances. The editor in chief of Gyldendal, Kari Marstein, took me down to the archives, and sure enough, we found a clean copy of the book, along with information about Tord Gusthjem, Brandeggen's editor. A quick check of the records revealed that Gusthjem was hired in the late summer of 1990 and that the only book he edited through to publication, before leaving the job over two years later, was none other than *Conglomeratic Breath*. I called him one day to ask him what working with Brandeggen was like, but as soon as I mentioned the title of the book, I was met with silence on the other end. Finally, he said, "I don't want to talk about it. I broke my back on that book, okay? I'm no longer in publishing." It was an uncommonly brief conversation. Brief, on the other hand, is the last word you'd use to describe the novel. At a ridiculous 2,322 pages, *Conglomeratic Breath* has the distinction of being, without question, the longest single-volume novel ever released by Gyldendal Norsk Forlag. The number of copies it sold can be counted on one hand. Apart from the twenty-five free copies given to the author, the one in the archives, and the thirty-two distributed to reviewers and booksellers, the remaining print run of 1,600 books was destroyed. This is not very hard to understand. The book is, in short, absolutely unreadable. Normally, I can appreciate books that push back against the reader, the ones that demand real effort, as long as they're well written. And at times, *Conglomeratic Breath* seems to fit that bill, as it showcases the author's exceptional linguistic perceptiveness, his virtuoso ability to navigate between multiple registers in a way that is very likely unparalleled in Norwegian literature. Nevertheless, the novel remains, for this reader, perfectly unreadable. Impenetrable, to an extent that frustration isn't even the right word. Next to this novel, Gaddis's *The Recognitions* and Joyce's *Finnegans Wake* (both of which Brandeggen read several times) look reader-friendly. It begins straightforwardly enough: the protagonist, with the trendy, alienating name of Imper Akselbladkvist, arrives at what he calls his house. He stands on the front steps, fishes for his keys, and enters once he finds them. This takes one hundred fifty pages. From there, it's full-on disintegration, until our level of disorientation becomes monumental and absolute. There are no paragraphs, no chapters, not even so much as a comma or period; at any given time, the identity of the speaker, when and where we are, what is happening and why, are all anyone's guess. For instance, Brandeggen devotes large parts of the book to exploring what he calls "the potential Heidegger-plagiarist level of the self," a notion every bit as perplexing as it sounds, which is made no more comprehensible by the fact that the starting point for these investigations is an old bedspread given to the protagonist by his grandmother. That is, two threads within the bedspread are the starting point, and the distance between them opens up entirely new vistas and a fresh round of investigations that themselves necessitate their own exploration for Akselbladkvist. As the text zooms further and further in, it deliberately and expressly assumes the structure of the Mandelbrot set, a fractal whose edge shows an infinite number of satellites, i.e., small copies of the original Mandelbrot set. To put it another way, soon enough, the reader is so deep into the details and the details of the details' details that not even the slightest glimmer of textual daylight remains. But then, somewhere around page 700, the text suddenly arrives at a light in the forest, a clearing. The reader's relief is enormous, almost indescribable, as Brandeggen gives us an unpretentious, affecting account of life on a street in Stavanger in the mid-70s. ⁜ This section becomes a small novel in itself, and a rather conventional one at that. A novel in which love and terror are forever living under the same roof, but the former always wins out in the end. Thematically and linguistically, it recalls the modern Scandinavian tradition of (rather more successful) coming-of-age novels, like Torbjörn Flygt's *Underdog*, Beate Grimsrud's *Tiptoeing Past an Axe*, Tore Renberg's *The Orheim Company*, and Lars Saabye Christensen's *Beatles*, even though only the last of these had come out in time to have influenced Brandeggen. It is not hard to imagine his editor pleading with him in vain to publish these 300 pages and scrap everything else. Nor is it hard to understand why the editor had had enough after this book. On page 1,009 the new story abruptly ends and the forest becomes thicker and more impassable than ever. The stitchwork of the text becomes tighter and tighter as Brandeggen weaves in more and more intricacies, setting a new standard for textual resistance and arousing an almost physical reluctance to read any further. As I strain myself to the utmost in order to drag my way through the unreadable, it becomes clear to me that the "novel" inside the novel, with all its rays of light and hope, resembles nothing so much as a nightmare, and that its only purpose is to underscore the impossibility of arriving and remaining in such a place in real life. Reality, Brandeggen seems to be suggesting, is the inexorable other from which we can never escape, where nothing is certain, and where every utterance opens into a chasm of doubt and new questions, which themselves open up even more doubt and even more questions that lead us smack into the Mandelbrot set once more. I gave up on page 1,700, more than six hundred pages away from the finish line, and never have I been more relieved to put down a novel.

⁂ Astra Road in Tjensvoll. A winding street with both detached houses and low-rise apartments.

156

[4] The only musical reference in the Red Handler books (with one exception) is to Glenn Gould's two recordings of the *Goldberg Variations*. This may have been a conscious choice on Brandeggen's part to emphasize the problem of duration and length vs. quality, which is further complicated by the fact that Gould's 1955 recording has a length of thirty-eight minutes, while the 1981 recording clocks in at over fifty-one minutes. In other words, a movement opposite to the one Brandeggen took in the Red Handler project.

[5] The three sentences dealing with the eyes are easy to dismiss as bland, even silly. But looking past their slapstick absurdity enables us to notice Brandeggen's critique of crime literature, in which novels often get needlessly prolonged (often by several hundred pages) and the reader's time wasted by the detective's failure to look closely and follow up on clues and hunches fast enough. To Brandeggen, the overwhelming majority of crime-fighting heroes were shockingly ineffective, in the sense that they coldly allowed the suspense to idle as the reader is led on—like the dog who follows a biscuit held by its owner as the latter moves further and further away—and were therefore unworthy of the fame they were customarily afforded. To his mind, the profusion of dead ends and suspects quickly became tedious. In these three sentences, on the other hand, the Red Handler a) identifies his problem and chief constraint (his eyes are closed), b) takes action and solves the difficulty (he opens his eyes), and c) is once again able to do his job in a prompt and exemplary manner.

[6] Note the complete absence of a murder mystery in this and several other of the Red Handler novels. Brandeggen consciously chose to break with the established rules of the detective

story, laid down by Van Dine and Knox, e.g., at the end of the 1920s. The private detective who only worked on murder cases, he reasoned, restricted the genre and alienated the reader, who presumably would be better able to identify with other types of crime, such as burglary, which deserved to be taken just as seriously given the major impact of these crimes on the lives of their victims. He had often read about families who were forced to relocate in the aftermath of a burglary, regardless of whether their abode had sustained any damage or whether the victims had been at home or not at the time of the break-in, simply because they now regarded their home as forever tainted with insecurity. Brandeggen also scoffed at Van Dine and Knox's unbending rule that the detective must never solve the crime as a result of blind chance, coincidence, or being at the right place at the right time. On the contrary, this became the Red Handler's modus operandi, given Brandeggen's deep interest in coincidence, the collective unconscious, and synchronicity. "Our reality is full of coincidences, or seeming coincidences. Linkages and undercurrents. Why shouldn't the Red Handler live in the same reality?" Brandeggen wrote in his notes. Again, he believed that reorienting the genre around a greater appreciation of people's lived reality would be key to the Red Handler's success.

[7] As early as the first Red Handler novel, the style has been perfected. The solution comes before the reader has a chance to get bored. Or, as Brandeggen himself wrote in one of his notebooks, in English (probably because he imagined presenting his concept to international publishers): *Crime fiction for the gentleman who loves crime novels, but hates reading.*

[8] The final reference to the Red Handler's wife, and one of only a handful to smoking. Brandeggen himself smoked constant-

ly and advocated for the greater social acceptance of *double-smoking* (inhaling from two cigarettes simultaneously) as something more than a party trick.

[9] The one exception to musical references noted above in the footnote about Glenn Gould. A possible nod toward the Saraghina sequence in Fellini's *8 ½*, a film dear to Brandeggen ever since he began frequenting the Stavanger Film Club, where he never missed a screening, yet always missed the chance to socialize with the other members.

[10] Brandeggen was very satisfied with this opening line. It was, according to him, "quite up to snuff."

[11] The phrase "in service to the people" is central to understanding the Red Handler. As readers we know that the Red Handler considers himself indispensable to the public, and since his work is altruistic and pro bono, the citizens gratefully acknowledge that everything he does is in service to the people. But those who have read more widely in crime literature may be puzzled when it comes to the Red Handler's crime-fighting mandate. Traditionally the private eye—i.e. an investigator with no official connection to the police—has no actual power to make arrests, and he can also be held legally accountable for meddling in and/or obstructing police work. Brandeggen devoted a lot of attention to this problem and for a time considered making the character a police investigator with an independent streak. In his notes to this novel, we find that Brandeggen rejected this solution in favor of an extensive origin story to explain how the Red Handler went from being a civilian vigilante (the notes mention Charles Bronson's character Paul Kersey in the 1974 film *Death Wish*) who took

the law into his own hands before running up against the police, who begrudgingly admitted the overwhelmingly positive
results of his efforts and accordingly—though reluctantly and
with grave misgivings—granted him a special private-detec-
tive license which permitted him to operate independently
and make arrests as long as he stayed within certain limits and
made regular reports to the department. Brandeggen made
several attempts to compress this story into something he
could include in the first Red Handler books, but eventually
chose to leave it out completely, either to avoid the text becoming too long and complicated, or (more likely) to also give
the Red Handler an air of the unknown, to press home the
fact that his origins were shrouded in mystery. The last novel
Brandeggen wrote—*The Red Handler Lands in Trouble with the
Authorities*—is therefore also better understood in relation to
this unused origin story, since the freedom the Red Handler
has been given eventually comes back to bite him and is re-
voked due to either unsubmitted paperwork or the incident
detailed in *The Red Handler and the Out-of-Control-Urine.*

[12] This is a remnant of the early, avant-garde Brandeggen: the
too-clever-by-half semicolon. Frode Brandeggen did not grow
up in a home with books. There were of course books in the
house—it would have been strange otherwise—but not enough
books, or enough books of a certain canonicity or undisputed literary merit, to call it a "home with books." Brandeggen claimed
he grew up with only one bookshelf, placed in one corner of
the living room and filled with photographs, knickknacks, and
potted plants, along with a small collection of books of the sort
that get passed down from generation to generation (Hamsun,
Kielland, Bjørnson, Undset, and the like), along with his father's
complete collection of Sven Hassel books, with pride of place

devoted to *Wheels of Terror*. There was also a well-worn copy of Jens Bjørneboe's *History of Bestiality* trilogy from which his father would read aloud when Brandeggen was little, especially at night in order to help the budding author fall asleep. Brandeggen told me, for instance, that his father would spend some weeks assiduously reading the trilogy's first novel, *Moments of Freedom*, out loud to him when he (F. Brandeggen) was five, and that he (F. Brandeggen) tremblingly fell asleep to the most hair-raising, terrifying accounts of human perversity and pure evil, from the slaughters perpetrated by the Conquistadors to the Salem witch trials to the rat-and-corpse-infested trenches of the Somme, Verdun, and Passchendaele to the rampages of Stalin and Hitler. "But," Brandeggen added, "I did grow to love literature." According to him, the young Frode Brandeggen's path to literature lay in a confusing mix of the desire to please his father by showing enthusiasm for books, and an equal desire to distance himself from the same man by seeking out literature he knew his father wouldn't like or couldn't understand. Even though he frequented the library's children's section with his mother to borrow comic books, Hardy Boys books, and the Famous Five series, he "upgraded" (his word) to the adult section and struggled his way through Swedish translations of Rimbaud's *Une Saison en Enfer* and Witold Gombrowicz's *Trans-Atlantyk* at the age of twelve, all under his father's disapproving eye. In his early teen years he plowed through tomes by Joyce, Pound, Barthelme, Cortázar, Perec, and Simon. When it came to Norwegian literature, he read Dag Solstad and everything by Ole Robert Sunde (the latter of whom he held in almost boundless admiration). Early in his literature studies at the University of Oslo (1990-1993) he became acquainted with Nicholson Baker's 1988 book *The Mezzanine*, a 140-page novel about a man going up an escalator, which included a long apparatus of digressive footnotes, one of which was a several-pages-long footnote about footnotes. This novel, Brandeggen would later claim, together with Claude Simon's *Histoire* (1968) and Ole Robert Sunde's *Kontrapunktisk* (1987), formed the triptych he would use in composing *Conglomeratic Breath*. As a student in Oslo, he also became absorbed by the nascent literary journal *Vagant*, reading every single issue from cover to cover. He attended all the readings, debates, and literary events he could—in a long herringbone coat and beret, the full regalia—and each time he went out the door, he dreamed of running into Alf van der Hagen, Pål Nordheim, Henning Hagerup, or one of the other members of the editorial staff. However, whenever he caught sight of them, he could not bring himself to approach them to introduce himself and ask whether he might send them one or two pieces. Brandeggen was at this time, and for that matter for the rest of his life, clinically shy. Apart from his dream of joining the *Vagant* circle, Brandeggen also dreamed of getting a cat, but he was too shy to ask the landlord whether cats were allowed. Instead he fed strays in the evening, on weekends. Otherwise, he divided his time between 1) studying, and 2) writing and studying what he'd written, by and large without talking to or seeing anyone else, sitting by himself in his flat on Sofies Street, where he began and three years later finished *Conglomeratic Breath*. Disappointed and demoralized over the complete lack of attention the book garnered among literary critics, he moved, tail between his legs, back to Stavanger in 1993. For good.

[13] Brandeggen believed that the "Show, don't tell" approach in literature had to be dispensed with if the Red Handler books were to reach their fullest potential. The reader, he reasoned, had much better things to do than try to guess what happened or

read between the lines. The alternative Brandeggen settled upon was, "Tell 'em like it is."

[14] A slogan of sorts for the *Légion Étrangère* (French Foreign Legion). A hint about the Red Handler's past prior to Haugesund? Brandeggen's connection to and interest in the Foreign Legion had its basis in Donald Duck comics.

[15] Brandeggen's notes for the novel include hundreds of reference photos of different types of basement flooring in all kinds of conditions and degrees of uncleanliness, representing a broad range of materials, such as concrete, untreated wood, water-damaged linoleum, ceramic tiles from Toscana, etc. The photos are accompanied by a number of fairly meticulous descriptions of the state of the material, with a particular focus on the presence of water, oil spots, plaster, rat droppings, as well as any damages, scratches, discoloration, etc. Given the amount of work devoted to researching and documenting the possibilities for the basement floor in this scene, it is worth noting that Brandeggen finally settles on—or reduces and consolidates his preliminary work to—this one word, which, curiously enough, captures it all: dirty. "The dirty basement floor."

[16] Note the innovative, compact mode of crime writing, however unfamiliar it may seem to the experienced reader. Brandeggen does not dwell on all the details, but hones in on the two most important pieces of information: 1) The length of the altercation, and 2) Whether the parties involved experienced it as dramatic or not. In this case: clearly dramatic.

[17] Brandeggen knew nothing about boxing. Nothing.

[18] A possible nod to Shakespeare, whom Brandeggen held in high regard. An aside, audible to the audience but not to anyone else in the text.

[19] What at first glance appears to be yet another bad joke, or an instance where the prolongation of textual time becomes an almost aggressive exercise in the Banalist style so characteristic of the Red Handler books, can also, in this case, be read as an example of what S. Robertzon refers to as "literature's hidden passageways" (see *Text as Maze: The Infinite Trap Doors*, Robertzon, et. al., 1977), as the three invocations of the word *Omega* lead us further and further away from the template (the crime narrative) and into what the author really wants to express (the hidden passageway, and the reformulation of Kant's *das Ding* as *der Schrecken an sich*). Worth noting in this connection is Brandeggen's handwritten notes to the novel, kept in a separate folder labelled Ω, or Omega, the final letter of the Greek alphabet. While all the Red Handler books are accompanied by notes on composition, characters, plot development, ideas for future expansion, etc., the notes to *The Red Handler Stumbles Across It* are remarkable both with respect to their length (142 pages versus on average 3–10) and in that only a few lines and keywords seem to be directly related to surface events in the novel. The lion's share consists of rather impenetrable material, all of it centering on a certain "Dr. Omega," with no indication of whether this was to be a character in the novel or whether it stands for an exploration of matters largely external to the novel and only therefore—for the sake of convenience, presumably—recorded in the notes for this Red Handler book. But the emphasis with which the word Omega gets invoked— no less than three times, and on three separate lines—strongly suggests a correlation between Brandeggen's thorough notes

and the inclusion of the word/concept in the final text. Even though the final text contains no explicit reference to any such character, much less a doctor. Instead, the extensive notes deal with various interpretations of the Omega concept and involve a good deal of mathematics. The most prominent of these, with thirteen mentions in all (five of them circled in blue ink), is the Friedman equation that defines density parameters within comparative studies of cosmological models. Reference is made also to the Omega point in eschatology, where Ω symbolizes the end to all existence. The Omega notes also take up what

$$\Omega \equiv \frac{\rho}{\rho_c} = \frac{8\pi G \rho}{3H^2}.$$

Brandeggen refers to as the Ω value, a factor related to what he (perhaps inspired by Hegel) calls "the presence of absolute Negativity," which is further contextualized by an extensive research apparatus regarding modern obstetrics and the responses given by new fathers at several European childbirth facilities from 1982 to 2012, all of which appear to deal with what can best be described as waking dreams or, for lack of a better word, sleep deprivation-induced visions, experienced by new fathers during the child's first twelve hours outside the womb. All of them shared certain similarities, such as the experience of a suddenly overcrowded (by people, midwives, doctors) delivery room, a red or reddish-brown switch/button on the wall by the door for the on-duty nurses, correlated auditory patterns upon the activation of said switch (white noise, steady footsteps that seem to come closer over a long period of time, up to twenty-four hours in subjectively experienced time), and an overwhelming feeling and/or unspoken experience of absolute negativity in the room. Common to all the men's reports is also the cataclysmic castration of the ego and of the genitalia at the conclusion of the "experience," usually carried out by a creature described as visually similar to the goat figure in Goya's *El Aquellare* (1821–23) and Éliphas Lévi's 1856 drawing of the Sabbatic Goat, with the words *SOLVE* (separate) and *COAGULA* (joined together) on the creature's arms, which relate back to the theme of the post-natal period and whom 72% of the men spontaneously and independently of one another identify as *Dr. Omega.*

The Ω value, Brandeggen insists, may be derived by considering a number of isolated factors that are more or less likely to influence one another: the time of birth, the weekday, the number on the door of the delivery room, the age of the midwife, the number of hours without sleep for the fathers prior to the "experience," the weight of the child, atmospheric pressure directly above the hospital at the moment of birth, and electrical discharges from cumulus clouds. By cross-referencing findings among the investigated factors, Brandeggen suggests that the potential for the "experience" increases the higher the Ω value, and is maximized in cases where the following factors align: a) childbirth between the morning hours of 1:22 and 4:48 on a Sunday; b) an odd number on the room; c) midwife's age < 30; d) sleep deprivation > 50 hours; e) birth weight < 4000 g; f) atmospheric pressure < 100.914 kPa / 1009.14 mbar / 757 mmHg / 29.80 inHg and rapidly falling, g) impending or present thunder.

[20] Frode Brandeggen took a substantial interest in Carl Jung, including his theories of human duality and the connection between the subjective and collective unconscious.

[21] Brandeggen considered the issue of the Red Handler's mode of transport for the longest time and from all possible angles. From the author's notes we find that he toyed with the idea of sending the Red Handler to the unnamed city in the novel—which we can assume to be Stavanger—by bus, boat, even plane. The advantage of a car, he reasoned, lay in the indirect freedom it afforded, along with the fact that the car remained inextricably connected to his past in Haugesund, where the car was registered and where the Red Handler resided for many years. The car, his old Opel, therefore turns up in several of the novels, as a reminder that neither crimefighting heroes nor the author can ever fully escape themselves.

[22] "That was already long ago" would have been a better sentence, but here the author grants himself a "poetic pause," as he often called it, with such syntactical liberties.

[23] Superbly vague, this. A reference to Haugesund, and a subtle hint. We realize he has been in Haugesund, and that something happened there. At the same time, we are left with an almost physical feeling that we don't know who he is, nor will we ever. This is most likely meant to evoke uncertainty in the reader. Can we trust the Red Handler? Can we have confidence in the unknown?

[24] Throughout this chapter, the author seems to be insisting and hoping that he has finally broken the surface and can breathe in the artistic air without being pulled back under by previous

false steps. There is something fundamentally tragic about this emphatic insistence, this deluded attempt to convince himself.

[25] Brandeggen gives us a disturbingly complex portrait of the Red Handler, a man who has every reason to drink himself to death, but who comprises self-discipline and self-destructivity in equal measure. He lives on a knife edge.

[26] Nothing to highlight here. An unambiguous sentence about transport. The Red Handler moves from one place to another, and the author resists the temptation to fancy it up.

[27] But here's where things get turned up a notch. Brandeggen hints at the existence of a copycat/doppelgänger and synchronicity.

[28] And here he is. The Glimmer Man. We don't learn much about him, either; he remains a mysterious figure with unclear motives, not unlike Lee van Cleef's character Angel Eyes in *The Good, the Bad, and the Ugly* (1966), Brandeggen's all-time favorite film after *Incubus* (1966).

[29] Rather risqué words from Brandeggen, not to pique the interest of his male readers, but more likely to pave the way for the surprising turn of events in Chapter 4. But it is worth mentioning that, in addition to large quantities of crime literature, Brandeggen also consumed serial literature, dime-store novels, and erotica for housewives like *Fifty Shades of Grey*. We see traces of that here.

[30] Of course he did not. No one does. But he did have excellent hearing, which is likely what Brandeggen is going for here.

[31] A flirtini consists of vodka, champagne, and pineapple juice. Some also use redcurrant juice. Not many, but some.

[32] She would, she would not, she would, she would not, it hurts, it doesn't hurt. This dance between the sexes. Impossible to make heads or tails of.

[33] The woman comes with an airtight alibi, and for a moment we suspect that the Red Handler has botched things up by suspecting the wrong person.

[34] Hmm.

[35] Classic male postcoital behavior: Fornication now out of the way, back to business.

[36] A rather unusual choice by Brandeggen: detailing the Red Handler's process of deducing the murderer's identity.

[37] Fortunately we come back relatively quickly to the inevitable conclusion and the consequences that follow.

[38] Touché! As if he is saying: "You're nothing to me. You're one out of a sea of women." The line separating the world of the Red Handler and that of the criminals is absolutely unbreakable.

[39] Here we get the murderer's motive. Even though, strictly speaking, we don't really need to know it.

[40] Here it is indicated that the Red Handler is a skilled driver.

[41] I.e., it is the Glimmer Man whom the Red Handler sees here. Exquisitely subtle.

[42] An instance of reversed mirroring? Brandeggen was known for dutifully reading user manuals cover to cover, regardless of what they were for. And he took a keen interest in technological innovation. On the other hand, he seldom spoke, and with very few people.

[43] No one knows who Bernt is. None of the notes to these novels mentions any Bernt. The only Bernt we know with any connection to Brandeggen is Dr. Bernt ████, who treated Brandeggen when he was admitted to ████████████████ ████████████. He was a good guy. He wanted the best for him.

[44] As it happens, Brandeggen hated breakfast and never ate it. Instead, he smoked and drank coffee as a protest against conformity.

[45] See *The Red Handler Hot on the Trail*, where our title character experiences an initial setback in forgetting to open his eyes, with nearly fatal consequences.

[46] And here we get the coffee. The Brandeggen Special. No milk, no sugar.

[47] Brandeggen owned a bathrobe. He used it often. He should have owned two so he could alternate, he often complained.

[48] One of Brandeggen's signature moves in the Red Handler universe: the criminal's immediate confession to the crime. The

experienced reader may well find it simplistic and unlikely, but Brandeggen does this for a reason. The goal is to pare away all the interminable pages devoted to the investigation, which would have led to the same outcome regardless: the bad guy's reckoning with justice. In his new, more concentrated mode of crime writing, Brandeggen compresses several hundred pages down to a line or two. And it must be said that this was how Brandeggen wanted the world to be: honest and coherent.

[49] Note how skillfully Brandeggen maintains the narrative suspense and thrust of the Red Handler's investigation without sacrificing brevity. He allows the first suspect to be a dead end, but the hunt is immediately back on.

[50] Again we see Brandeggen simply point out the drama in the text instead of dragging it out through long descriptions of the hero's retching and wild gesticulations.

[51] And here he reveals that the danger is over and the reader can relax—for now.

[52] He tells it just like it is. No nonsense.

[53] This is here presumably to give the reader something to identify with. We've all had the experience of burning our toast. As it happens, moreover, Brandeggen's father was given a sandwich press by his sister for Christmas in 1979, with which he burned his thumb so badly on December 30th that he was unable to take part in New Year's Eve festivities the next day. He sat inside, looking from all the fireworks to his bandaged thumb while everyone else sat next to him in silence. No words were exchanged by the family until around midday on January 2nd.

[54] Again, we see traces of Brandeggen's avant-garde roots: not until Chapter 5 do we learn that it was this aunt who gave the Red Handler his sandwich press.

[55] Yellow symbolizes danger.

[56] And *thus* the case is masterfully resolved.

[57] This is the point where, according to his notes, Brandeggen found himself in a dire predicament, since he had no dictionary at hand, nor did he want to get dressed to go to the library while he was making such good progress on his novel. Most of the nine pages of notes for this novel have to do with this challenge, or as he calls it, "the crisis."

[58] Fortunately the crisis was averted by his use of the word *plates*. But he chose to leave in the problem around dishware/dishes, to remind himself of how hairy things could get.

[59] This might seem like an idiotic thing to have your character say, but Brandeggen has no qualms coming across as prosaic and unintentionally funny (in keeping with the French school of Banalism, see note 177), which allows him to condense a thrilling narrative about the criminal's preparations for the big heist. Five words are all it takes to convey the robber's meticulous planning.

[60] Brandeggen was not unfamiliar with street slang and wanted to demonstrate the Red Handler's command over the harsh reality he inhabited, hence "the joint" here instead of the far more conventional "prison."

[61] Here we sense that the author's frustration spills out into the novel itself. In his despair at this fresh problem à la dishware/dishes in the form of cup vs. mug, Brandeggen feels he is losing control over his own text, which in turn leads to his hero's violent outburst.

[62] And now back to the sandwich press. Poor Brandeggen. He just can't let it go.

[63] Had Brandeggen managed to stay closer to his original intention, this entire paragraph would have been omitted to start the novel right away with what is now Chapter 2. Strictly speaking, this paragraph is unnecessary. But he loved the description of rain here.

[64] He apparently had the film *Gremlins* (1984) in mind here, in which catastrophe ensues when the moderately cute mogwais are exposed to water. He was a big fan of this film.

[65] This would obviously have been a much stronger opening line for the novel. No time wasted before we find ourselves at a possible crime scene.

[66] See the next footnote.

[67] A healthy individual's field of vision stretches approximately 90° from side to side, 60° in toward the nose, 60° upward and 70° downward. The notes to *The Red Handler and the Musical Bandit* reveal that Brandeggen did extensive research on the eye's form, functioning, and diseases, and that a twist in the novel was to involve the Red Handler suffering from glaucoma. He likely

decided that such a twist would have needlessly complicated the novel.

[68] Initially the publisher Gyldendal thought that several words must have been omitted here by mistake, but on closer inspection (along with recourse to the author's notes), it is evident that this is yet another Brandeggen Special, for the dash here serves the double purpose of criticizing excessively long sentences and of hooking the reader at a moment of utter suspense in the sentence immediately following, where the suspect turns toward the Red Handler.

[69] There are multiple references to rain in the Red Handler novels and Brandeggen's notes. Some will attribute this to the noir tradition and authors like Raymond Chandler and Dashiell Hammett—whose influence on Brandeggen is obvious elsewhere—but it is more likely due to the fact that it rains a lot in Stavanger, and even more copiously in Brandeggen's part of town.

[70] Woah!

[71] Of course not, why should he? It's just rain.

[72] Indeed.

[73] Brandeggen wasn't afraid of clowns. But he was afraid of children.

[74] This line also appears in the manuscript of the proto-Red Handler novel *Randa Simulacrum Malignum* (see note 243).

⁷⁵ Much could be said about Brandeggen's use of the Ferris wheel as an element of suspense, but the reader deserves the chance to enjoy these electrifying passages without further interruption from me. Let it be noted simply that Frode Brandeggen never visited an amusement park as a child. What follows is therefore a result of meticulous research and multiple interviews with people who had been to amusement parks.

⁷⁶ The observant reader will notice that this is the only reference to Løkken Beach and the Jutland peninsula in the Red Handler universe; in all other instances, the protagonist's nostalgia and memories are connected with Copenhagen and its environs. It should therefore be noted that the only foreign vacations Brandeggen ever took growing up were to Løkken Beach, also known as "the Danish Riviera," or as the ad put it, *"a place where the white shores are endless, as is the range of thrills and fun activities for the whole family."* For Brandeggen, however, the only thing that was endless about the twelve summers he spent there was each long, lonesome day. Like his detective hero, Frode Brandeggen always wanted to visit Copenhagen, even if just for one day, but his parents never granted his wish, saying, "If we wanted to experience traffic and crowds, we might as well stay home." Ironically enough, Brandeggen almost never travelled abroad as an adult, and the few times he did so, it was exclusively (apart from his later trips to Dresden) to North Jutland and, well, Løkken Beach. He never went at the same time as his parents.

⁷⁷ This condescending, stigmatizing description of the carnival worker can only be attributed to views instilled in the author by his parents.

[78] Apropos of North Jutland and Løkken Beach: Brandeggen's parents missed his funeral, with the excuse that they had already paid a nonrefundable deposit on a bungalow right next to the water.

[79] Frode Brandeggen owned only one suit his entire life. He paid for it with the advance he received for *Conglomeratic Breath*. The only time he ever wore it was to his own funeral.

[80] Clearly a reference to the ideal length of a Red Handler novel. But also a hidden reference to Brandeggen's brief musical career, which spanned from the spring of 1986 to the fall of 1988, when he was the lead vocalist and primary songwriter for Vaginal Wipe, the postpunk band whose songs rarely lasted longer than a minute and a half and which played both of its only shows at the Tjensvoll Recreational Center. After that the band members went their separate ways.

[81] Cold as ice. But with a hint of something ritual, like a blessing offered to the dead, not like the traditions that have been passed down by the Comanche tribe in the United States.

[82] The words "could have been perceived as" carry considerable significance. The Red Handler may not necessarily regard the murderer with sympathy, but the possibility is there. Ambiguity prevails.

[83] According to the notes, this novel was completed on March 13, 2013. On the last few pages the author has hastily scribbled the words Løkken Beach, an address, something that looks like a reference number, and the dates July 8-15. From this it appears

likely that Brandeggen spent a week in North Jutland in the summer of 2013.

[84] Brandeggen was more than a little pleased with this sentence. For a time he toyed with the idea of opening all the novels with it. But it was not to be.

[85] A possible reference to Sebastian "der Wasserdoktor" Kneipp (1821–1897), given that Brandeggen had in the fullness of time given hydrotherapy and the so-called "Kneipp Cure" a chance. In the handwritten notes to *The Red Handler and the Secret Massage Studio* as well as the first draft, Dr. Omega appears in place of Dr. Kneipp.

[86] Of Brandeggen's many interests over the years, parkour was probably the one that occupied him most throughout his adult life. ⁂ Much of the credit for this goes to a Briton named Michael Bjørn Edwards, one of the few people in whom Brandeggen confided to some extent. They first met somewhat by chance, but at a decisive time for both men. Michael had come to Norway because of love, gotten a job in the oil industry, begun a career, and was getting on well in life. Then it all went wrong: his wife left him for a wife of her own and he fell victim to his company's layoffs. Michael felt adrift. At this point a random internet discovery led him to parkour, which would help lead him out of his life's ruins. As one of the sources he found put it: "Parkour *is a sport in which the object is to get from A to B in the most efficient way possible. When a* traceur *(practitioner of parkour) comes to a fence, rather than seeking the nearest gate, he or she will look for the most effective way of overcoming the obstacle. Parkour is not a competitive sport, that is to say, competition is not part*

of its essence. Insofar as there is competition, it is with oneself and no others. The object is constant improvement, to overcome one's own limitations. The discipline of parkour was invented by a French child named David Belle together with some of his friends. The friends later went in a different direction than Belle. A totally different direction. Disagreements arose. This was distressing for all concerned, no question. Far too many taunts—even hurtful and downright uncalled-for missives—were passed between them via go-betweens on small bits of paper, The boys' parents called a meeting to stage an intervention and clear the air. No one came. Everyone was outside jumping all over the place. Some with tears in their eyes. A sad time, just truly, truly sad. One of these friends, Sebastien Foucan, a.k.a. Foucen [f'okkan] began a similar discipline called freerunning. This was not well-received by David, to put it mildly. He was furious. Began tearing down the walls of his bedroom. David and Foucen no longer spoke or passed notes to each other. They no longer communicated at all except by cussing. Anyway: whereas the object of parkour is to get from A to B in the most efficient way without interruption, freerunning *allows one to stop and perform electrifying moves like spins, somersaults, and other acrobatics. Since a somersault* (salto mortale) *can hardly be described as an efficient move, it is not considered part of parkour."* Michael had no interest in impressing others or doing gymnastics. Pragmatics over aesthetics, was his view. Discovery, humility, and personal freedom over perfection and finesse. He was in perfect alignment with David Belle's "philosophy," a word that is here used deliberately in quotes. In all modesty. Michael began using words like *vault, discovery, precision, tic tac,* and *wall run* in entirely new ways. He bought sweat clothes and good shoes and changed his name to simply Michael Bjorn. Now there was no stopping him. He explored his own personal freedom and parkour as a way of expressing his inner pain. Parkour is a state of mind, not just a collection of moves,

2-DISC SPECIAL EDITION

DISCOVER PARKOUR WITH MICHAEL BJORN!

EDGE
TO
EDGE

"IT'S OUTSTANDING!"
ROGALAND TIMES

IT'S JUST AN EDGE, BUT IT CAN BE YOURS.

■ **EDGE TO EDGE** ◄

When Michael Bjorn Edwards lost both wife and job within a short time, he veritably fell apart. Feeling shipwrecked, he spent day and night on Sola Beach, alternating between trying to learn how to surf and looking wistfully across the North Sea for a glimpse of his beloved England. But the weather was never right, neither for surfing nor spying land. It was a long way home (in every sense of the word) and he was slowly suffocating within the stifling architecture of the city. He had to do something. It was then that a random internet discovery changed everything. Michael discovered parkour, and at once the sharp edges of life and the city were no longer a problem to be solved, but an opportunity to be seized. He changed his name to Michael Bjorn, bought sweat clothes and running shoes, and with that he was off. It was the beginning of a new beginning. A life. A new opportunity. He became: The Parkour Man.

In this instructional video, Michael Bjorn takes you on a journey across a town you thought you knew, teaching you to see new possibilities everywhere.

"It's just an edge,
but it can be yours."
- Michael Bjorn

Edge to Edge: Discover Parkour with Michael Bjorn!
Subtitles: Norwegian, English, Chinese (Cantonese) // Audio: Dolby Digital 5.1
Running time: approx 240 min. + extras / Year of production: 2016 / Sport

©2016 Michael Bjorn Productions
Distributed by Lumnicfilm

PG-13 PARENTS STRONGLY CAUTIONED

Some strong language, intense sequences of free-running and frequent airing of grievances.

Some Material May Be Inappropriate for Children Under 13

he explained. It was just as much about overcoming mental and emotional obstacles as physical ones. But while Belle and his followers emphasized the fastest way of getting from A to B, and while devotees of the freerunning idiot glorified the aesthetics of motion and extreme stunts, Michael Bjorn was fascinated by the rough edges that constituted the boundaries of the city just as much as his own life, and how these edges, instead of remaining obstacles, could be used for something positive. He formulated this in what he termed "Edge Philosophy," which he explicated in a volume entitled *Life on the Edge: The Parkour Man* (self-published, 2012) and an instructional DVD, *Edge to Edge* (Michael Bjorn Productions/NRK Rogaland, 2013). The main thesis of Edgeism is that, in Michael's words, "Everything is edge. Stairs are edge. Edges are edge. It's just an edge—but it can be yours. And you will find edges all over town." For Brandeggen, Michael Bjorn was a person who showed how limitations could be used to explore the ego. To him, the chiseled-down Red Handler books represented the edges of literature.

⁂ This, as well as the board game Dragster (MB/Premier Toys, 1982). Frode Brandeggen was ranked #12 globally and considered nearly unbeatable when he played with the blue cars. Reidar (#62) was his preferred opponent and Guileless Gary the obvious choice of referee.

[87] "You are too good, Red Handler" was long the working title of the first book in the series, which later became *The Red Handler Hot on the Trail*. Later on, "You are too good" became a recurring feature of the Red Handler novels, a catchphrase of sorts. The intention was (as Brandeggen explained) "to create a world where logic won out in the end and where everyone could agree about the essence. The essence of my Red Handler novels is simply that the Red Handler is too good, the criminals don't stand a chance, and therefore, the novels cannot be any longer than they are. I guess you could say I wanted everything in black and white. Probably."

[88] A mystery, plain and simple. Brandeggen reveals nothing about the massage studio, not where it is, the services it offers, nor what relevance it has for the characters and the novel as a whole. The only thing he does point out is that the characters never say a word about the establishment. And, faithful to his characters unto the last, the author keeps his mouth shut, too.

[89] Brandeggen too suffered from insomnia and for a time self-administered his own cocktail of 10mg Imovane® (zopiclone), 5mg Stilnoct® (zolpidem) and 0.5mg Rivotril® (clonazepam) and/or 5mg Valium® (diazepam).

[90] The same was true for Brandeggen. People often called him butterfingered. For he *was* butterfingered.

[91] Again, the same was true for Brandeggen.

[92] Brandeggen later berated himself for not being able to think of a better word than "splash" here. He struggled with this sentence for eleven days. But it was all in vain.

[93] Surely it is impossible to be caught more red-handed than this. But this sentence is worth a whole chapter in itself for the extraordinary amount of suspense it contains. What will happen now? Will the murderer turn himself in, or point his weapon at the Red Handler?

[94] Once more we can observe the author's mastery of narrative technique. Neither time nor suspense gets wasted. The use of the word "intense" causes us to veritably quiver with anticipation when we come to this line. It *is* intense, and that is how it must be. That's crime fiction for you. Intense. Relentless.

[95] Perhaps an expression for Brandeggen's desire for a coherent and predictable world, but the murderer's empathy and acute concern for the victim's well-being also makes for an interesting twist.

[96] Running ensues. But not so fast that they risk falling down and injuring themselves. A taut, precise sentence.

[97] A possible case of Stockholm Syndrome. But impossible to say for sure. The author dangles the possibility and lets ambiguity prevail, in the best spirit of crime fiction.

[98] The case is solved and order restored. The author often felt ill at ease if he left off the text while anything remained unresolved for any of his characters. He preferred to conclude on a note of amicability, if not friendship in any real sense.

[99] Despite the harmony we get at the end, Brandeggen felt obliged to remind us that all was not well for the girl, even if the crime was solved. As if to reinforce the theme that everything had consequences.

[100] Brandeggen was always fascinated by the fact that there were more dead people than living.

[101] Also meant metaphorically, i.e., in the Red Handler's life? In Brandeggen's? Perhaps.

[102] Here we note Brandeggen's unwillingness to use the word "elegant," and how he skirts the problem by writing, "Elegant, almost." Itself an elegant move.

[103] The BBC series *The Singing Detective*, with Michael Gambon in the starring role as a bedridden crime author suffering from severe psoriasis, Philip E. Marlow—who drifts in and out of a hallucinatory, Raymond Chandleresque universe—made a strong impression on Brandeggen and can be considered one of the main sources of inspiration for the Red Handler project. Brandeggen especially admired the series' constantly evolving plot, its dreamlike tendencies, and the fact that no solution to the mystery was ever revealed. The observant reader who thoroughly examines both *The Singing Detective* and the Red Handler novels will find a smorgasbord of cross-references. This is not the place to go further into them, so I will confine myself to pointing out the importance of the alter ego motif in both works, and the way in which Marlow's preoccupation with his mother mirrors Brandeggen's (unjustified) guilt complex toward his own mother. It is also interesting how Alison Steadman plays both Marlow's mother and the murder victim

"Lili" on the show. Freud is undoubtedly lurking just behind the curtains.

[104] A bit of self-deprecating humor. Brandeggen himself applied for a patent for medicinal hot-dog water (Patent no. PCT/NO2009/03587). The product was never put into production.

[105] Sometimes we can only applaud Brandeggen for his love and enthusiasm for the Red Handler, which is on full display here. Brandeggen was not a happy man in his final years, but it was moments such as these—where he was surprised by his own crimefighting hero—that made it worth going on. We more readily forgive, therefore, the disproportionate celebration of the open door, even though he (Brandeggen) exercises some restraint in pointing out that two "bravos" are enough.

[106] Classic salesman rhetoric. Brandeggen despised traveling salesmen of all shapes and sizes. The whole novel can therefore be read—indeed, it is nearly impossible not to do so—as one long vendetta.

[107] What at first glance appears to be a bit of crude fat-shaming humor on the part of Brandeggen—and which, God knows, absolutely *can* be taken as such—is more likely an attempt to create a sense of foreboding, later compounded by the salesman's rejoinder that "Things happen all the time. To anyone." It could just as well be Brandeggen's way of conveying that everything now is in a state of precarious, unpredictable flux, below the surface of facile appearances.

[108] In Brandeggen's notes we find out that the Red Handler actually owned two smoke alarms. Why he claims to have only one, is anyone's guess.

[109] The Red Handler is a bit naïve here, at least through German lenses. In April 1997 the daily *Frankfurter Allgemeine* reported that as much as 34% of the population lied about their bathing routine, in order to appear more, how should I say it, hygienically disposed.

[110] The classic inability to accept a refusal. This salesman and that drunk guy at the bar have a lot in common.

[111] Now, wouldn't that be something.

[112] This final foreshadowing statement veritably sucks us into the next chapter.

[113] An indication that Brandeggen knew what he was talking about. Hot-dog water and musty houses have a not-dissimilar odor.

[114] *"I'm sure I'll take you with pleasure!" the Queen said. "Two pence a week, and jam every other day." Alice couldn't help laughing, as she said, "I don't want you to hire me—and I don't care for jam." "It's very good jam," said the Queen. "Well, I don't want any to-day, at any rate." "You couldn't have it if you did want it," the Queen said. "The rule is, jam to-morrow and jam yesterday—but never jam to-day." "It MUST come sometimes to 'jam to-day,'" Alice objected. "No, it can't," said the Queen. "It's jam every OTHER day: to-day isn't any OTHER day, you know." "I don't understand you," said Alice. "It's dreadfully confusing!" "That's the effect of living backwards," the Queen said kindly: "it always makes one a little giddy at first—" "Living backwards!" Alice repeated in great astonishment. "I never heard of such a thing!" "—but there's one great advantage in it, that one's memory works both ways." "I'm sure MINE only works one way," Alice remarked. "I can't*

remember things before they happen." "It's a poor sort of memory that only works backwards," the Queen remarked. From *Through the Looking-Glass, and What Alice Found There*, Lewis Carroll (Macmillan, 1871).

[115] In case he wasn't already, the Red Handler becomes our hero and our man. He does what so many of us always dreamed, but never dared.

[116] The Red Handler never banks on anything he can't hold in his hands.

[117] But he is also a man who gives a thought to the future. Along with incorporating the Microsoft scam, Brandeggen gives a nod to climate change in order to add a touch of contemporary relevance and societal awareness. No man is an island, etc.

[118] It is interesting how often the criminals in these novels seem relieved at being caught red-handed. As if our hero is the one who brings deliverance, and that this explains the almost jovial tone that prevails after the crime is brought to light. An early name of the Red Handler was the Nabber, implying one who not only solves crimes and makes arrests, but also embraces. The person who is nabbed is also held close. In a sense. Moreover, crime can be seen as the very image of a person who has crossed a limit. In this light, the Red Handler becomes a version of the savior who rescues people from darkness. It is almost as if Brandeggen is trying to prevent himself from fully stepping over that line.

[119] Almost as a note to himself within the novel, Brandeggen points out that it is unnecessary to say it a third time.

[120] A reference to *The Red Handler and the Glimmer Man,* where we learn about the Glimmer Man's name plate.

[121] A glimpse of the detective's career at its earliest inception.

[122] Classic setup . . .

[123] . . . and classic payoff.

[124] It is likely that the use of the term "master detective" twice in the novel is a slip on the part of Brandeggen, a trace of his fraught childhood in which Astrid Lindgren's series of books about Kalle Blomkvist, Master Detective (released 1946–1953) was one of the few bright spots. He read all of them several times before obtaining what would later become the highly sought-after Swedish pamphlet *How to Become a Master Detective* (1955) to train himself in the art of Blomkvistism, or "Crimefighting for the Common Man," as it was also called. The foreword to the pamphlet reads: "It is in society's best interest to raise each individual to be a good citizen. Quite often, however, the developing youth is led astray, making it all the more necessary to step in to instill positive values in him or her. A lot of time and money, to say nothing of effort, has gone into ensuring the best possible foundation for today's youth. Our social workers have been assisted in their work by the police, and their combined efforts have already shown clear results in many cities. Community centers have been established for film screenings, lectures, and hobby clubs for young people." For Brandeggen, Blomkvistism represented a way to impart meaning and logic to existence. If, as a teenager, he lost interest in the life of a detective as he turned his attention to serious literature and culture in general, including the avant-garde in all its various guises, he would return to

his boyhood fascination with the intractable mystery when he took up the Red Handler project and, per usual, read everything he could get his hands on about the subject. Sir Arthur Conan Doyle was a natural touchstone, although Brandeggen was never particularly enthusiastic about Sherlock Holmes (apart from, one might argue, the obvious influence on the figure of the Red Handler, especially given how the Red Handler is always seeing connections and identifying the culprit long before everyone else does—indeed, it is as if we are all the time expecting him to pronounce, "It's elementary"). He also read Collins's *The Woman in White*, Gaboriau's *Monsieur Lecoq*, and Poe's "The Murders in the Rue Morgue," "The Purloined Letter," and "The Mystery of Marie Rogêt," again without any special reaction or revelation. Brandeggen derived much more from the noir tradition and hardboiled detective literature from the 1930s to the 1950s, including *Perry Mason Solves the Case of the Glamorous Ghost* (Erle Stanley Gardner), *No Good from a Corpse* (Leigh Brackett), *Honey in His Mouth* (Lester Dent), *Bunny Lake Is Missing* (Merriam Modell), *The Golden Gizmo* (Jim Thompson), *The Maltese Falcon* (Dashiell Hammett), *Dark Passage* (David Goodis), and, last but not least, Raymond Chandler's *The Big Sleep* and *The Long Goodbye*. The last of these struck a particular chord with Brandeggen due to the personal element it contained; Chandler's presence in *The Long Goodbye* is unmistakable, and he had written it in a similar state of mind as Brandeggen, namely, on the brink of depression, overconscious of his own shortcomings, beginning to suspect that all his writing amounted to very little, and finding the whole endeavor of literature nigh impossible. Frode Brandeggen, more from a self-imposed sense of duty than anything else, also took a deep dive into contemporary crime fiction of the last 10 or 15 years or so. It was this that solidified his aversion to certain of these authors' detours, their tendency to drag out the plot over hundreds of pages or, even worse, several books, even as he admitted that certain representatives of the genre were welcome exceptions to the rule. For instance, he held the Harry Hole novels by Jo Nesbø in some esteem for the way they developed or adapted the Chandleresque, and for the level of aggression these books contained, though it is safe to assume he believed Nesbø could've easily pared it down in some places. At a particularly low point, Brandeggen toyed with the thought of contacting Nesbø and proposing a collaboration, but, as so often before, shame and the fear of rejection prevented him from doing so. Nevertheless, it is hardly going too far to suggest that Nesbø's success was a considerable motivator for Brandeggen's work on the Red Handler.

[125] Overt media criticism here.

[126] Shiny LipSlicks from Cover Girl was the brand, according to Brandeggen's notes.

[127] Brandeggen purposely lets the recipients of these gifts remain a mystery. One might assume that the aunt from *The Red Handler and the Great Diamond Heist* is among them, perhaps also the old flame, or even the mysterious Bernt. But all we can do is speculate; presumably, Brandeggen wanted merely to hint at rather than trumpet the idea that the Red Handler had any close relationships.

[128] An early draft of this sentence ends thus: "... and no one had told him, like maybe a new episode of *Father Brown*." Brandeggen had never seen the show, but knew of it.

[129] Always on the alert, always.

¹³⁰ Brandeggen's love of cats was well known. This would change suddenly in 1999.

¹³¹ There it is again: the semicolon.

¹³² TrioVing AS is a Norwegian manufacturer of locks and fittings. The company was founded in 1864 and is today the nation's leading supplier in the industry. The name consists of Trio (a merging of Christiania Doorhandle Factory, Stavanger Armature Manufactory, and Skien Ironworks) and Ving (consisting of Christiania Steel Mill and P.W. Rosenvinge). In 2004 TrioVing was bought out by the Swedish conglomerate Assa Abloy (itself a first-rate manufacturer, to be sure).

¹³³ This is based on a real dream Brandeggen had in 1999, though the top hat was originally a flat cap. One evening at my residence in Dresden he related his riveting dream about the unhappy cat who dreamed of journeying to America by steamship.

¹³⁴ Burmese cats are known for their disproportionate size/weight ratio. It is uncertain whether Brandeggen was aware of this, since much of this scene seems to go beyond realism and into *das Unheimliche*. ⁂

    ⁂ The concept of *das Unheimliche* (the uncanny) can be traced back to Sigmund Freud in his 1919 paper of the same name, where he identifies it as the point where the familiar coincides with horror, thus confronting the subject with the unconscious and the repressed. The French psychoanalyst Jacques Lacan expanded the idea by suggesting that *das Unheimliche* places us "in a position where we no longer can distinguish good from bad, pleasure from unpleasure." See also Julia Kristeva's notion of *abjection*.

[135] Never before has the process of cogitation and reasoning been presented so succinctly as in these three lines. Hmm.

[136] See the novel *The Red Handler on Vacation in Denmark*. Our man likes to travel.

[137] Here we are witness to a genuine moment of despair for the Red Handler. He works himself to exhaustion to keep the city safe, but is always one step behind the relentless onslaught of crime. As if he knows the day will never come when the last criminal is behind bars. A Sisyphean career, in every sense of the word.

[138] It continues to gnaw at him, this moral dilemma. Collaging exerts a strong pull, and many a man has cowed under its spell. Such a simple craft, such exquisite results.

[139] On the alert again. Only for one moment does he allow his thoughts to wander.

[140] The notes for this novel contain photographs and detailed descriptions of different curtain patterns Brandeggen considered specifying in this passage. In the end he decided to leave it to the reader's imagination.

[141] Self-control wins out. The hobby can wait till later.

[142] For this sentence Brandeggen did extensive research on the regulations for sole proprietorship/self-employment, and his

notes contain an overview of the unique challenges within this employment category, such as the requirements for accounting (if not financial auditing), the lack of sick leave and pension accrual, and other problems such as the inability to claim the minimum standard deduction unless the sole proprietorship is formed into a corporation with oneself as the sole employee in order to become an ordinary wage worker and thereby qualify for the deduction, etc. He found the rules for value added tax rather byzantine, and the final novel, *The Red Handler Lands in Trouble with the Authorities*, might indicate that the VAT problem has come to a head, alongside the income tax. On the one hand, the question is whether the Red Handler's activities are subject to VAT if he does not accept any pay for them, and on the other, whether nabbing crooks is not also a service he gives away free of charge, and whether in that case he assumes a tax liability in the first place. And so on.

[143] Only a detective like the Red Handler can allow himself to be so offensive. But he knows what he's doing.

[144] Note this highly unusual (for Brandeggen) exchange in which the suspect first concedes he has been caught ("Hmm . . . you are too good . . . too good") before he backtracks, attempting to escape incrimination by sowing doubt about his marital status. Only to be found out again ("Damn. You got me there, for sure").

[145] The Red Handler keeps his cards close to his chest. As readers, we know he can back up this assertion.

[146] True enough.

[147] The plot, one might say, thickens.

[148] Here I am. Here. *Me.* The time has come for me to step forth and make an appearance in my own person. A necessity, given the circumstances. For the very first time. A first time for everything, and just as inevitably a last time for everything, a last time that is forever invisible to the one at the center of the event, the experience. I stood on a beach in Cape Le Grand National Park in Western Australia, a good 30 miles east of Esperance; it's been twenty years since I stood there alone one morning and vowed I would return someday. But I never did. I even remember how I avoided taking it all in, determined as I was to save something for "next time." A next time that never came. Only a "last time." I have been east of Esperance (50 km), for the last time. Almost everywhere I've ever gone has been for the last time. Now I sit here, shut inside these footnotes, doing the work of annotation that has occupied me for as long as I can recall. Year after year, book after book. They send me the books with a request to supply footnotes, annotations, interpretations, insights. Time and again I've done as I'm told, always an advisable course as long as you don't know any better. Here, I must ask the reader's pardon, as I've yet to introduce myself; my manners have unfortunately fallen into the sere with time, a byproduct of the product I supply, where the focus has always been the work of others, while I stand in the shadows of my masters, so to speak. However, I've not only dwelled, but thrived in those shadows, for it is there the light shines brightest, as I've often said and/or believed and/or thought. In darkness we become visible to ourselves. That's why I've always preferred dark offices, heavy, dark-stained wooden furniture, dim lighting, the curtains drawn to (or preferably no curtains at all, only walls) to ward off all distractions. No interruptions. No surprises. Predictability, always predictability. The most beautiful of all words. Every day like the one before it, and nary a ripple on the surface of the

water. Ah, here I go again: I'm guilty of omission, squeezed in by digressions, led astray from my promise to step out of the ranks and into the light, if only for one moment. To show my true face. So without further ado: I hail from Augsburg, in Bavaria, from Datschiburg, from Aux; it all depends on whom you ask. If you were to ask me, I would tell you I come from here, and that my name is Bruno Aigner. My mother's name was Cesia. I could tell you that I first saw the light of day in 1934, and ever since that time the darkness has only grown thicker. No, that's all I have to say, all I can say; I would prefer to go by the Footnoter, as I'm known among clients, I almost said my fellow men too, but that would have been an acceleration of the truth into the orbit of the lie, where the speed only increases and increases toward a singularity of falseness. I have always, always striven to banish all falseness from my work and in my life, those inseparable quantities, two sides of the same coin. Ack. What was I going to say? My fellow men have never known me as the Footnoter. My fellow men have never known me, period; I am just as alien to them as they are to me. It's best that way. For all involved. Involvement is never without peril, as you risk being unable to outvolve yourself again; a progressive entanglement (≠ development), revolution, revolution, it's how I keep going in my dark room, carefully emulsifying the words until they bubble up and separate and have to be mixed together again. And yet and yet and yet. Over sixty years the maker of annotations, the annotator, I don't know what they've been calling me, only accepted the jobs they give me. Out of a sense of duty, I've gone to my mailbox and carried the manuscripts inside, expanding upon them from within with my impressions. I'm supposed to breathe life into them, contextualize them, set them into relief, concretize, problematize, examine. A multitude of different vantage points as dictated by the publishers' cover letters,

194

written by office assistants just as anonymous as I am. Never have we met, our exchanges have been confined to the letters on the page. *Blah blah blah*. One day I'm going to write a footnote where that's all it says, it'll be my finest moment, the only time I'll ever remember having laughed. Sixty years, 443 annotated titles. This is number 444, and my last. I began with Fischer's thirty-year anniversary edition of *Der Zauberberg*. It was I who revealed Thomas Mann's tendency to prefer the back entryway, so to speak. Even though Anthony Heilbut would take the all the credit, forty years later, for throwing the doors to the Mannian closet wide open. As if that were something to take credit for. And after? After that, more. After that, Beckett and Bove and Bernhard and Bradbury; Bellow, Baudelaire, Blixen, Backmann, Baker, Blake, Ballard, Bataille, Blatty, Böll, Borges, Brome, Bjørnson, Bull, Brontë, Brown, Bukowski, Burroughs, Burgess, Byrne, etc., etc., etc., Brandeggen. For some reason, all the authors of my books have had names beginning with B. With the exception of Mann. Probably a test, a journeyman's test of some kind. You'd think there'd be annotators for all the other letters of the alphabet, and that someone is out there making sure we never cross paths. The letter *B* became my territory. // My parents brought me to America as a five-year-old. My father called it a permanent vacation. Only several years later did I learn about this Austrian chap who'd taken over my country and caused a great stir, but by then I'd already taken to my father's vacation idea and the way it fit so well with the American spirit of freedom, and I hoped the Austrian would never go back to where he came from so that we'd never have to do the same. We stayed. And I wish I could say I made myself deserving of the perpetual vacation that was paid for with lives in the KZs, but that is not the case. Quite the opposite. Instead of accepting the sense of obligation my mother attempted to instill in me, I took my father's vacation mentality to its furthest logical conclusion, deciding, at the age of sixteen, to become a hobo. A vagabond, that is, a wanderer. For six years I sailed the seven seas of cargo-train routes throughout America, armed only with a bit of sausage and what at that time were still my good spirits. My father, farseeing and supportive as he was, followed me to the train station the first day, took my photograph, and wished me the best of luck. It was a scene at once affecting and exceedingly strange. *Auf Wiedersehen*, he said. *I'm a ramblin' man*, was my reply. We had long ago developed our own separate languages. You might think it was somewhat reckless of my father to send me on my innocent way at sixteen, but we both agreed that the fact that I looked much, much older was insurance enough for the journey. I looked nearly forty, and was quite proud of it, I might as well add. This unusual maturity of mine (if you can call it that) had

long had its advantages, such as the fact that I had already, at the age of twelve, debuted sexually with women up to twenty years my senior, and had spent an extraordinary summer of 1946 in Oregon, celebrated as I soon was by the ladies of Salem for my boyish disposition. My libido in those days was tremendous. It is, like so much else, gone now. // I lived on the rails, eventually developing a mutually dependent (and unhealthy, said Jonny Carl) relationship to the banjo that more than once supplied food for the two of us at the time of our sorest need. It was Jonny Carl who introduced me to the hobo signs that we long navigated by and that soon sparked my fascination with the sign as such, its universality, the inherent possibility of language to illuminate itself. I stole my first books in the fall of 1955 someplace far up in Montana, including a copy of William Blake's *The Marriage of Heaven and Hell*. Soon I was filling it in with my annotations and footnotes, which so irritated poor Jonny Carl that we soon went our separate ways, and not at all amicably or quietly, some distance outside Bismarck, North Dakota, one year to the day before I tumbled out of my last train and stumbled into Pennington, Minnesota, the birthplace of my fledgling footnoting career. It was here I met Knut Johnsen, who inspired me to pursue Norwegian, this almost impossible language I slowly learned to love, its orthographic abominations and all. A hard language, like a wrench you'd use to repair a delicate Swiss watch; I had to learn to use it with care and ingenuity, it seemed impossible, an impossible and unusable language. I fell quite in love with it. After the baton was passed to Nixon and silly season reigned across the United States, I returned, tail between my legs, to Germany and settled in Dresden, a city that no longer existed, except as an approximation formed out of the ruins of what it used to be before the bombing and firestorms destroyed everything. I've been here ever since, apart from the

You can camp here	Kind lady lives here	Barking dog here	Kind gentleman lives here
Vicious dog here	Nothing to be gained here	Good place for handouts	Will give to get rid of you
Police arrest hobos on sight	Doctor here won't charge	Owner is out	Owner is in
Authorities are about / alert	Good place to catch train	Man with gun lives here	Not a safe place

HOBO SIGNS

regular trips to Norway I always looked forward to after meeting Frode Brandeggen. That's all I have to say, for now. Except that this work has been my greatest honor, to be able to dive in and live among the Brandeggen's boiled-down art, in which I, for once, at long last, can permit myself to write subjectively, to lift up the author in my own way, according to how I see fit, the way I think he deserves, without shame, without the imposition of some arbitrary limit on the number of annotations, without fear of an employer whose first concern is selling books or mollifying students, professors, reviewers, and other sundry connoisseurs of critical editions. For once, an opportunity to step forward and show my face, to hold the reader's hand until we've arrived at the destination. At a certain point in time, I think I recognized the need for it, to emerge from the crowd, out of anonymity, as this, in all likelihood, would be my one chance to ensure the Red Handler novels are understood and appreciated like they deserve, despite everything. Despite everything.

[149] Incredibly, the Red Handler finds a solution, another gambit, in this situation too. Brandeggen's writing here is breathtaking.

[150] "Too good for your own good." With my hand on my heart, and not without some bitterness, I can say the same was true about Frode Brandeggen.

[151] Smart in a way that verges on the metaphysical. The logical underpinnings begin to give way here and the reader is forced to reflect on the paradox. But again, not in a way that would be too difficult or time-consuming.

[152] A shocking outcome. But also ingenious.

[153] And there we have it. A split within the character of the Red Handler.

[154] Here Brandeggen is plainly trying to confuse us and evoke a sense of noirish disequilibrium: Is the Red Handler listening to the early or the late recording of Gould's *Goldberg Variations*? We never find out, for Brandeggen purposely leaves us to feel the doubt in our very bones. Simply magical.

[155] Brandeggen's contribution to dirty realism, or what has been labelled the genre of gutter crime fiction. If there is any-where the author goes too far, it is in this description of the cat. It is totally unnecessary to the story and only adds need-less suffering for mere shock value. But perhaps Brandeggen included this literary gut punch precisely in order to show his

restraint in other places, or perhaps he felt the need to devote a few words to why his love of cats came to an end in 1999, when he witnessed something similar and was clawed in the face when he tried to help.

[156] Again, we get no answer, no indication of what the Red Handler is thinking. The question is left superbly open. Goddamn, that's good.

[157] This is a highly calculated and shrewd attempt on the part of Brandeggen to recall the preceding Red Handler novel, making the reader feel as if they have missed out on something important if they didn't read *The Red Handler and the Unsolvable Mystery of the Burmese Cat*. A kind of "collect 'em all" feeling the author clearly wants to arouse in the reader in order to maximize the series' commercial (but also artistic) potential. It is hardly coincidental, then, that a cat should turn up in this novel as well. Interconnections. Always interconnections, associative links.

[158] This may be Bernt again. No one can say. This novel really is chock full of mystery and insinuations.

[159] A whiff of Beckettian or Pinterian dialogue here?

[160] Eros in the air. Along with the murderess of *The Red Handler and the Glimmer Man* and the old flame in *The Red Handler on Vacation in Denmark*, this woman completes a kind of erotic triangle in the Handlerian universe.

[161] It is here established beyond doubt that the story takes place on a Saturday.

[162] Brandeggen introduces and reinforces the Yiddish atmosphere by incorporating the word *oy* (from *oy vey*) instead of its Norwegian cousin *oi*. The latter of which is, of course, derived from none other than *oy*.

[163] Brandeggen isn't making all this up.

[164] It's unclear to me why the rabbi would say this. Unless he believes it is Friday, which is not outside the realm of possibility. In that case, the sabbath would lie ahead of them.

[165] After the long intermezzo from Rabbi Mandelspritzer we are thrown brutally (and, I think it's fair to say, thankfully) back into the blunt reality of the heist plot.

[166] The drama reaches heights here that are almost intolerable. I need a cup of tea. One moment. All right, I'm back.

[167] By the way, I'm having Schweizer Gut'Nacht Tea from Ricola. There must be someone out there who'd like to know that. ⁂

> ⁂ If there was one thing about Frode Brandeggen, it was that the man drank too much tea. Way too much. That was on me, by and large.

[168] Previously, the assailant was too busy plundering to notice the Red Handler. But now the Red Handler, for his part, is too busy putting handcuffs on the assailant to come out with an appropriate quip.

[169] Yiddish: "A curse upon your whole life." Or something like that.

[170] Brandeggen was an avid reader of *Tex Willer* and toyed for some years with the idea of writing a series of sexy Westerns in the vein of Kjell Hallbing's Morgan Kane series.

[171] It is entirely fair to ask whether *The Red Handler and the Difficult Sabbath* ought to have been left out of this collection. It is certainly an outlier. The length is one thing, while another is the structure of the novel itself, with its long, slow passages and the conciliatory mood that prevails at the end. The very first chapter signals that we are in for something quite different, contemplative, brooding. The Red Handler's spirit is troubled, an element of doubt or hesitation has crept into the character. And, to many a reader's surprise, he has become a Jew. It is almost impossible not to read this in connection with Brandeggen's own religious musings during this period. It is almost as if he is using the Red Handler to write his way through something, and we might read the text through a therapeutic rather than a purely commercial or artistic lens. But are all three understandings of the text possible at once? Absolutely. Toward the end of the first chapter, the intrigue gets introduced with a bang: the phone rings. The tension is starting to build. But then Brandeggen takes it back down a notch. Secure in his own powers of narration, he allows Chapter 2 and the lengthy Chapter 3 to play out in the company of Chaim Mandelspritzer. Chapter 3 is especially notable for the way it delves into the Jewish rules for the sabbath. God knows it is all very interesting from a purely religious standpoint, but more to the point is how Brandeggen seems to be pursuing two different strands at once. For one thing, the rabbi's endless enumeration of the Jewish laws becomes a trope for conformity, the societal landscape the Red Handler continually must navigate in his line of work, which, in that sense, has nothing to do with Judaism per se, of

course, so much as the private detective's eternal dance with the authorities and their various representatives who would force the Red Handler to conform with their rules. Another way to frame it would be in terms of edges, the edges of the system or of existence, and how the Red Handler chooses to use them either as boundaries or springboards. Not only that, but while the rabbi drones on with his analysis, brooking no interruption, the clock is ticking for the detective, who becomes more and more anxious he'll miss the imminent robbery. By reminding the reader what time it is at regular intervals, on top of making the clock go much faster than the rabbi's monologue would lead us to believe, Brandeggen manages to imbue this seemingly dry sequence of events with a breathless anticipation whose equal one would be hard-pressed to identify in all of literature. In this way the novel's length itself becomes an element, a device in its own right. The Red Handler is running out of time, and we readers are losing both time and patience, but time can never be stopped. Time must go on, the case must be solved. Most of us are familiar with the notion of a "race against time," and Brandeggen unleashes it here to an extent perhaps unlike any of the other Red Handler books; but though this novel might depart from French Banalism's limitations on length and plot development, and though it might seem weaker than the others in this collection, it nevertheless contains a value all its own, and we recognize the author's courage in introducing the great question in a crime novel: Who do we want to be? And in light of the resolution to the case, remarkably conciliatory yet depressingly uncompromising (the Red Handler first shows sympathy for the perpetrator, only to then tell him that we never escape who we truly are), along with the novel's pseudoreligious ending (our detective breaks bread with a baker he doesn't know, acknowledging that he is once again merely, for better or worse, the Red

Handler), we can only applaud Brandeggen for shedding light upon *the human condition*, in all its garishness.

[172] Until gentrification permanently altered this one-kilometer road, Isted Street was known for its cheap hotels, drug dealers, adult movie theaters, and prostitutes.

[173] Another example of Brandeggen's gift for economy. When the hero is asleep, there is no need to add anything until he wakes up.

[174] Nowhere else do we get any mention of brewer's yeast. It is possible to view it in connection with the hot-dog water in *The Red Handler and the Travelling Salesman Who Didn't Work for Microsoft* and the protagonist's occasional concern for health and wellness.

[175] He is wearing a hat.

[176] And why describe it otherwise? Yet again, Brandeggen shows us how precise he can and will be.

[177] This sentence is a good example of Banalist literature, from which Frode Brandeggen drew much inspiration and is the school of literature to which the Red Handler books most clearly belong, if only with mixed success. ❋ Banalism, or the *Mouvement artistique du banalisme* (MAB), as it was officially called, was established by Jean-Claude Camille and Thierry Beauchamp in 1971 in the wake of Camille's novel *Salut! Voici mes pieds* [Hello! Here Are My Feet, 1970] and Beauchamp's *Un homme heureux avec un chat et un chapeau—et autres histories* [A Happy Man with a Cat and a Hat—and Other Stories,

1971], in which the title story consists, in its entirety, of the following:

L'homme porte un chapeau. Le chapeau est sur sa tête. Le chapeau est doux, ça le rend heureux. Il est également heureux quand il regarde son chat. Son chat a le poil doux, plus doux que son chapeau. L'homme est plus heureux quand il prend son chat que quand il prend son chapeau. Il est encore plus heureux quand il caresse son chat en portant son chapeau. Là, il est très heureux. Alors il fait les deux en même temps. Il est super heureux.

The man is wearing a hat. The hat is on his head. The hat is soft, which makes him happy. He is also happy when he looks at his cat. The cat's fur is soft, softer than the hat. The man is happier when he touches the cat than when he touches the hat. He is happiest when he pets the cat while wearing the hat. Then, he is very happy. So he does both at the same time. He is super happy.

MAB, largely unknown and even less chronicled outside of a narrow band of avant-gardists in France and the United States (where Walter Hopping's *Garbled Love* [1972] and *Evol Garbage* [1974] are considered foundational Banalist works), differs from Naïvism in that it is far more aggressive and uncompromising. Less the pursuit of a lost childhood or a simpler past than a contestation of the liberal, capitalist order that exalts anti-intellectualism and the easily digestible over aesthetic merit, Banalism aims to unmask those who would water down artistic complexity in all their garishness and vulgarity. In this way, it shares certain traits with Dadaism, but diverges by cultivating not irrationality, nonsense, anti-reason, and anti-logic, but rather, for lack of a more convoluted way of putting it, the commonest of common sense. ✣✣ The Banalists had the idea of reaching into the very core, the origin of art and literature, stripping away all embellishment until nothing remained but the elementary particles. ✣✣✣ Even the letter in itself was extolled as the most basic representative of the literary reproduction of the world, as shown by the Russian author Paramonov Vladislav "Slava" Yaroslavovitch in his novel *A* (1927), whose back cover announced a poignant, heroic tale of one man's struggle to lead his aging and beloved bull Pasha home from work in the forests by the Nizhnyaya Tunguska River in Siberia after an accident. As a text, however, the novel consisted solely of the letter A, which appeared once, on the book's first (and last) page. The movement's adherents aimed to put the banal on full display, exposing the seams that held it together so that those very seams could be unraveled. Such a scorched-earth tactic, it was hoped, would eventually yield something of value, a content that could not be scraped away even at the most basic level, which could therefore, beyond giving the banal work a de facto value in itself, create a stepping stone for new, more complex forms. ✣✣✣✣ In this way, Banalism takes on a somewhat altruistic and seppuku-inspired character as it surrenders all ambition to the success of future artists. Certain literary scholars have pointed to the Swiss literature collective Gruppe Olten, in particular Peter Bichsel's books *Eigentlich möchte Frau Blum den Milchmann kennenlernen* [And Really Frau Blum Would Very Much Like to Meet the Milkman, 1964] and *Kindergeschichten* [*Stories for Children*, 1969], as an important model for MAB. A blow to the movement came in 1976, however, with Hopping's untimely passing; in France, meanwhile, Camille and Beauchamp struggled to maintain support and visibility for MAB. They officially threw in the towel in 1982, after eleven years and over fifty releases, with the bittersweet joint edition of *Pas de pieds, pas de chapeaux, pas de chats* [No Feet, No Hats, No Cats] and *Rien de rien, et merde*... [Nothing from Nothing, Goddammit]. Jean-Claude Camille moved to Algeria and settled in Algiers, while Thierry Beauchamp remained in Paris and found a job with RATP. At regular intervals over the years that followed and as late as 2003, seemingly new, home-printed MAB-affiliated books were found on the platforms of the Porte de Clignancourt and Simplon metro stations in the 18th arrondissement, an area where Beauchamp's address was registered.

⁂ The Banalism referred to here is considered the original school, and must not therefore be confused with the later use of the term within the visual arts (represented, e.g., by the Polish artists in the Ladnie Group), architecture, politics, etc.

⁂⁂ The *Dada Manifesto*, read aloud by Hugo Ball at a Dada soiree in Zürich on July 14, 1916, shows clear points of similarity with what later became the Banalist movement (indicated here by boldface): "*Dada is a new tendency in art. One can tell this from the fact that until now nobody knew anything about it, and tomorrow everyone in Zürich will be talking about it. Dada comes from the dictionary.* **It is terribly simple.** *In French it means 'hobby horse.' In German it means 'good-bye,' 'Get off my back,' 'Be seeing you sometime.' In Romanian: 'Yes, indeed, you're right, that's it. But of course, yes, definitely, right.' And so forth. An international word. Just a word, and the word a movement.* **Very easy to understand. So terribly**

207

simple. *To make of it an artistic tendency must mean that one is anticipating complications. Dada psychology, dada Germany cum indigestion and fog paroxysm, dada literature, dada bourgeoisie, and yourselves, honoured poets,* **who are always writing with words but never writing the word itself, who are always writing around the actual point**. *Dada world war without end, dada revolution without beginning, dada, you friends and also-poets, esteemed sirs, manufacturers, and evangelists. Dada Tzara, dada Huelsenbeck, dada m'dada, dada m'dada dada mhm, dada dera dada, dada Hue, dada Tza. How does one achieve eternal bliss? By saying dada. How does one become famous? By saying dada. With a noble gesture and delicate propriety. Till one goes crazy. Till one loses consciousness. How can one get rid of everything that smacks of journalism, worms, everything nice and right, blinkered, moralistic, europeanised, enervated? By saying dada. Dada is the world soul, dada is the pawnshop. Dada is the world's best lilymilk soap. Dada Mr. Rubiner, dada Mr. Korrodi. Dada Mr. Anastasius Lilienstein.* **In plain language**: *the hospitality of the Swiss is something to be profoundly appreciated. And in questions of aesthetics the key is quality. I shall be reading poems that are meant to dispense with conventional language, no less, and to have done with it. Dada Johann Fuchsgang Goethe. Dada Stendhal. Dada Dalai Lama, Buddha, Bible, and Nietzsche. Dada m'dada. Dada mhm dada da. It's a question of connections, and of loosening them up a bit to start with. I don't want words that other people have invented. All the words are other people's inventions. I want my own stuff, my own rhythm, and vowels and* *consonants too, matching the rhythm and all my own. If this pulsation is seven yards long, I want words for it that are seven yards long. Mr. Schulz's words are only two and a half centimetres long. It will serve to show how articulated language comes into being. I let the vowels fool around. I let the vowels quite simply occur, as a cat meows . . . Words emerge, shoulders of words, legs, arms, hands of words. Au, oi, uh. One shouldn't let too many words out. A line of poetry is a chance to get rid of all the filth that clings to this accursed language, as if put there by stockbrokers' hands, hands worn smooth by coins. I want the word where it ends and begins. Dada is the heart of words. Each thing has its Word, but the word has become a thing by itself. Why shouldn't I find it? Why can't a tree be called Pluplusch, and Pluplubasch when it has been raining? The word, the word, the word outside your domain, your stuffiness, this laughable impotence, your stupendous smugness, outside all the parrotry of your self-evident limitedness. The word, gentlemen, is a public concern of the first importance."*

✱✱✱✱ The elementary particles, or, as Brandeggen's Norwegian fellow author, Dag Solstad, formulates it, "the insoluble epic element." The question is obviously, on the one hand, how much Solstad was familiar with and influenced by the MAB when in 2013 he released the (to some) unreadable (and to others) masterpiece *The Insoluble Epic Element in Telemark in the Period 1591–1869*, a novel that, all the while insisting that it is a novel, likewise insists on relating the author's family

Here we see Hugo Ball in character as the Magic Bishop at the Cabaret Voltaire in 1916, in a public performance of his poem "Karawane," which consisted entirely of nonsense words.

history and nothing else in the time period in question for over 460 pages, without chapters or any other divisions along the way, without detailed psychological portraits of any of the characters, without any descriptions of time or place, indeed without anything other than the barest details from an endless array of village chronicles and genealogical tables, all in the name of getting at "the heart of the matter." In any case, we know that Brandeggen read what critics dubbed Solstad's "Telemark novel" with great interest (a tattered copy lay under the author's bed) and closely followed the polarizing reception the book was met with. ⊗

⊗ On the novel's title page, Brandeggen wrote, "*Un-effing-believable!*" probably because he realized that the Telemark novel was everything *Conglomeratic Breath* never became: an uncompromising literary work of enough significance to be discussed and debated. Or perhaps because Solstad's novel also partook in the same sort of reductiveness that characterized the Red Handler project, while benefitting from a whole different level of virtuosity, and within a different sort of oeuvre altogether. Inside Brandeggen's copy were also several reviews of the novel with certain passages underlined, such as the one from Amund Børdahl in the Norwegian literary journal *Vinduet*, which appeared a few months before Brandeggen's passing in 2014: "*As critics have pointed out in several of the leading dailies, Solstad's writing borrows from the*

'logic and vocabulary' (Aftenposten) of genealogical research and occasionally resembles 'the countless
village histories written by local patriots and published by small presses throughout rural Norway'
(Dagbladet). But, and without diminishing our
country's tradition of the encyclopedic village chron-
icle, Solstad's prose is of a whole different caliber
than our celebrated history writing from town and
country. It is composed with a syntactical musical-
ity so that we may to speak, as the reviewer from
VG put it, of a "symphony of names." A genealogical fugue, or, if you will, the Telemark variations,
less a collection of personal or historical facts (valu-
able though they may be to some) than a work of
art. The fate of generations running through the
text gets lifted above the merely private and local to become a small, nay, a great cross-section of
Norway's history, in the form of a wide-ranging,
fictionless poem, 'carved directly from time' . . .
Among the reviews of the Telemark novel, we find
the following assessments: 'unbelievably boring,'
'a litany of genealogical minutia,' 'detail-obsessed,
flat, maddeningly stuffed full of the names of people
and farms and villages and years and dates,' 'go-
dawful as a novel—but a blast as genealogy goes,'
'poorly edited,' 'It had no editor, this book, I can only
conclude,' 'Was no editor available?', 'It doesn't seem
edited at all, really,' 'Any other author and the book
wouldn't have been published,' 'almost unreadable,'
and, writes one of them (while excluding themselves): 'There's not a reader alive who can read this
stuff.' Several of them agree, either in irritation or

satisfaction, that it amounts to an 'anti-novel' or else that the 'gleaning of information from family trees and village chronicles is hard to stomach and can scarcely be characterized as a novel' . . . *'To give you, this novel's potential audience, a taste of the impossibility of the task before you,' writes one of the reviewers, 'allow me to cite at random from one of the book's 457 pages: "Anne Ellefsdatter's mother was Ragnhild Gregarsdatter Ryen, whose first marriage was to Ole Taraldson Melås and was mother to the abovementioned Anders Olson Melås, but also to Torgrim Melås, and who married Torhild Vreim, who'll be described later, as well as to Harald Melås, who married Taran Torsdatter Skoe, which makes her another one of my ancestors."* // From Frode Helmich Pedersen's reply to Børdahl's review, Brandeggen underlined the following: "*Solstad's point, in short, is that the capitalist system has gnawed its way so deeply into the publishing industry over the last few decades that the novel as such can no longer avoid the demand to entertain. The fact that his latest novel was met with 'mockery and scorn' is therefore seen as symptomatic of an age in which readers become indignant when presented with a novel that doesn't entertain them. An attractive analysis, but does it hold up? Are those of us who disliked the novel really the victims of a capitalist ideology that has eaten its way into our brains without our noticing? Or could it be that all the resistance has more to do with the book itself and its various aesthetic flaws? . . . Even Solstad himself, in the public lecture he is*

213

currently touring the country with, admits that of course this novel is reader-unfriendly, before immediately pointing out that almost the entire modernist canon of narrative prose consists of reader-unfriendly novels, which to him stems from the fact that the novel in this time period (1890–1960) was absolved of any duty to entertain . . . For instance, it is absurd to accuse Solstad of arrogance, of being a kind of literary feudal overlord, of indulging his need for dominance. Solstad, of course, is perfectly entitled to do whatever he wants, and, of course, is hardly to blame if his publisher is willing to go along with it. This isn't the work of a hack, nor is it quite simply a bad novel—to be honest, I'm not even sure we can call it a clear-cut case of an experiment gone wrong." ¢

¢ One thing is, however, painfully clear: Brandeggen's own sense of the inferiority of *Conglomeratic Breath* in relation to *The Insoluble Epic Element in Telemark in the Period 1591–1869* is on-point and probably correct. The same thing is true for how the novel succeeds in (read: carries through with) its uncompromising aims, compared to the Red Handler novels, which fail to consistently follow the ideals of the MAB, therefore striding an uneasy split between an avant-gardist inflexibility and reader-friendliness. Brandeggen knew of course better than anyone that Dag Solstad was an author of a whole different caliber than himself, which he acknowledged in a humble letter to Solstad in 1993. A letter that, moreover, went unanswered.

✳✳✳✳✳✳ The earliest hints of Banalism in literature can be traced all the way back to the first sentence in the first chapter of Cervantes's *Don Quixote*, where the author makes it clear from the beginning that the geographical location of the action about to take place is inessential to understanding (and enjoying) it: *En un lugar de la Mancha, de cuyo nombre no quiero acordarme, no ha mucho tiempo que vivía un hidalgo de los de lanza en astillero, adarga antigua, rocín flaco y galgo corredor.* In Tobias Smollett's 1755 English translation, this sentence reads thus: *In a certain corner of la Mancha, the name of which I do not chuſe to remember, there lately lived one of thoſe country gentlemen who adorn their halls with a nifty lance and worm-eaten target, and ride forth on the ſkeleton of a horſe, to courſe with a ſort of a ſtarved greyhound.* Having said that, the rest of Cervantes's novel, along with the second volume published ten years after the first, has little to do with what we would identify as Banalism. The same can be said, to put it mildly, about Sterne's *The Life and Opinions of Tristram Shandy, Gentleman* (1759), in which Brandeggen took a keen interest from time to time. In this fictional autobiography, penned by a protagonist given to digressions and completely

unable to explain anything in a simple, straight-
forward way, the hero does not arrive at his own
birth until the fourth volume.

[178] By the way, the stuff I wrote earlier about Australia is made
up. I've actually never been. Probably I just wanted to make myself seem important. But the other details—the masturbation,
Gone with the Wind—are correct.

[179] We never find out more about the old flame than this, the
fact that she lives in Copenhagen. To be sure, we do learn in
The Red Handler and the Unsolvable Mystery of the Burmese Cat
that she uses/used lipstick, but who she is, how and when she
met the Red Handler, and the nature of their shared past, all of
this remains a secret between the two of them. So to speak. The
notes to the novel do contain an extensive background story set
on the Greek island of Hydra, where an early case of the Red
Handler's involves a vanished stove, among other things.

[180] This is probably the same mint pastille the Red Handler
wanted to buy at the start of the second chapter of *The Red Handler Stumbles Across It*, even though it is there described much
more prosaically as a "mint."

[181] The murderer caves under the onslaught of the Red Handler's questioning. We are quickly whisked into the explanation
phase of the novel.

[182] The Red Handler, in telling the murderer what gave him
away, exposes himself in a sense by giving such an unimpeded
view into his investigative methods. But since it'll be a long

time before this criminal sees the light of day, we know it can't hurt.

[183] Once I had a thought about a zebra that was licking the glaze off a garden hose while it showed me its collection of exotic garden gnomes. Isn't that strange? It lasted only a moment. Then I thought about something else.

[184] Here Brandeggen is speaking in his own voice, unfortunately.

[185] The Red Handler slept in the nude. Sometimes in a pair of white underwear. But most of the time nude. (Author's notes to the novel.)

[186] This gives an idea of Brandeggen's own increasing isolation in the last few years of his life.

[187] Here we see a trace of the Brandeggen of *Conglomeratic Breath*. He gets hung up on the language used to describe the problem of the doorbell, and the novel threatens to run aground before it has even gotten underway.

[188] Fortunately he opens the door and the drama can begin.

[189] Again, we don't know. I don't know.

[190] The doppelgänger. Classic literary trope.

[191] "Fake Red Handler" was, for a long time, the working name for the character who would become the not-Red Handler. Brandeggen always got a kick out of a good negation.

¹⁹² Who, when, where, how, and—last but not least—why, remain unclarified. Brandeggen doesn't dwell on it. In any case, the Red Handler is aggravated by an old bullet wound.

¹⁹³ For the longest time I was convinced I was the only one Frode Brandeggen had shown the Red Handler manuscripts. Certainly I would have remembered if he had ever mentioned showing them to anyone else. I was greatly surprised, therefore, some years after Brandeggen's funeral—and in connection with the work of annotating this volume—to receive a letter from the Norwegian film director Arild Østin Ommundsen. This letter revealed that not only had he and Brandeggen crossed paths several times during Frode's lifetime, but that Østin Ommundsen had also been sent the manuscripts, which had significantly influenced a new film he was working on. Østin Ommundsen offered to come to Dresden to show me a working copy of the film, which I naturally accepted. Together, we spent an afternoon and evening in an autumnal Saxony, and when Arild showed me his film, I could not help but be moved by how much of Brandeggen I saw in it. Even though I'd been told what to expect, I was deeply affected when I saw Brandeggen speak as a character in the film, even if he was played by an amateur who did little to illuminate the man himself except by dressing in the same manner as my friend, the forlorn author. As this connection shows the impact Brandeggen had on the people he met—and that his project was not nearly as hopeless as he believed toward the end—and since some readers will surely want to explore the relationship between the novels and the film, with Østin Ommundsen's blessing I include parts of the letter I received from him: (. . .) One November evening in 2014, I fell off my bike and hit my head on the edge of a cobblestone street. My right

ear was practically split in half. I'd been working hard the past few weeks and was looking forward to turning in early. But that of course didn't happen. I spent the night at the hospital instead. The evening had taken an unexpected turn, one would say. Over the next few days, I lay thinking about similar experiences I'd had. Nights of fateful choices and chance encounters that led into almost nightmarish circumstances. The first of these was in London one night in 1986, when I was sixteen. Due to a situation involving an Italian girl, I found myself wandering the city by myself. During that night I was taken for a male prostitute, had to flee from a gang of hooligans, and ran into a strange sorceress in a park, before finally finding my hotel sometime around sunrise. Later that year I saw two films that reminded me a lot of my own experience that night: Martin Scorsese's *After Hours* and David Lynch's *Blue Velvet*. It was after the screening of *Blue Velvet* at Filmteateret in the fall of 1986 that I first met Frode Brandeggen. He was my own age, and I remembered seeing him around town since he stood out from everyone else. He walked around in a long winter coat and green rubber boots in all weather. And he smoked. Constantly. Sometimes two cigarettes at once. *Blue Velvet* made a huge impression on me. I stood outside Filmteateret feeling almost faint after what I'd just experienced. "How about a double smoke?" said a voice in the night. Frode held forth a blue pack of cigarettes with a drawing of a horse on the front. "Yeah, it's Blue Master, but that's meant ironically." I didn't know what he was talking about, but took one anyway. My first cigarette ever. It felt like the right evening to take up smoking. "David Lynch, though, am I right? Jesus Christ," I said. Or something to that effect. We stood there smoking and talked. About how that film was unlike anything we'd ever seen before. We talked all night. About Freud. About what "lurks just under the surface," about Dennis Hopper, who'd directed *Easy Rider* but had since become an addict, about how Lynch's previous film, *Dune*, was a masterpiece despite its many flaws, or perhaps because of them. Later I threw up all the nicotine I'd taken in. I'd never met anyone like Frode before. He'd seen films I thought I was the only one who'd seen at my age: *Eraserhead. Sunset Boulevard.* Robert Altman's *Images.* Even ones I'd never heard of: *Kiss Me Deadly. Experiment in Terror. The Swimmer.* It was like opening a door into a world I knew existed, but never thought I'd find. After that first intense evening, I didn't see Frode Brandeggen again for over five years, though I tried many times to find him. I would hang out downtown in the evenings. Went to the movies and the film club often. But no luck. He was gone. As if that meeting had been a dream, and the night that had meant so much to me never happened. The next time I saw Frode was when I was studying at the University of Oslo in the early nineties. It was after a screening of Lars von Trier's *The Element of Crime* at the film club. I walked out into the night, feeling again like I'd just seen something truly special. And there he was. Frode Brandeggen. I recognized him immediately, huge beard and all, scrawny as he was at that time. I don't think he recognized me. Why should he? We weren't exactly old friends. And it was almost as if he wasn't there. His eyes looked dark and empty. He bummed a cigarette off me (Blue Master, quite unironically) and split. That was that. The last time we met was in 2006. I'd completed two features at that point, *Mongoland* and *MonsterThursday*, and had become a bit of a local celebrity back home in Stavanger. I'd just been to a Thomas Dybdahl concert at Folken and was taking a little walk before hooking up with the band, which included my girlfriend and now wife, Silje Salomonsen. He stood smoking in a small park. This time he recognized me. "Fifteen years ago, man," he said, holding out a pack of cigarettes (Prince Red). I took two. He knew all about my career in film and wondered when I was going to make something 'decent,' as he put it. I was a little insulted. He went on to say that he'd published some massive brick of a novel that he'd been working on in the nineties, back when I lived in Oslo. He was fascinated by the idea of synchronicity and said I should read Carl Jung, Erwin Schrödinger's book on metaphysics (*My View of the World*), and Arthur Koestler's *The Roots of Coincidence*. Which I only did many years later. He went on about how everything is interconnected, and how everyone you meet is a character in a narrative that is our own lives. How even the cashier at the grocery store can be a mentor, the woman at the welfare office a Guardian of the Gate. That sort of thing. I'll be honest and admit that most of it went straight over my head. In truth, I might have been thinking that this was a man who'd crossed a line. Walked through a door he should never have opened. It scared me to see him like that. A brilliant mind that, to all appearances, was falling apart. But there was still something there that fascinated me. A sense that he possessed some wisdom, had realized some essential truth. Something that lies right under everyone's nose, but that the rest of us somehow missed. Right behind the door nobody dares open. Brandeggen had paid the price for opening it. Those three meetings haunted me when, in 2014, I planned what became *Now It's Dark* while I lay recuperating. It was at this time I began receiving manuscripts in the mail with no return address. Stories about a detective who went by the Red Handler. I thought it was a humorous take on the crime genre, but didn't think much of it at first. But then I started to read and notice things in between the lines. What these texts really were about. I picked up on several hints that pointed in the direction of Brandeggen, strange turns of phrase I remembered from the way he spoke, the constant referencing of Glenn Gould. Things like that. The last envelope also contained a note that read: 'It is what it is. Here's hoping you're able to make something decent out of it, Arild.' It was then I knew for certain that this was the work of Frode. I started incorporating elements of the novels in the screenplay to *Now It's Dark*. And I wrote a scene with a character named Frode Brandeggen as a kind of tribute to the guy who had meant so much to me, even if I'd only spent a few fleeting nighttime hours in his company. It all seemed to fit in with the kind of story I was trying to tell. It all seemed right. P. S.: One more thing. The last thing Brandeggen said to me, that last night in 2006, I think he even hugged me as he said it, was: "I see miracles everywhere, Arild, you get what I'm saying? People, you know. They're all right." (. . .)

[194] But who, who? The reader quivers with anticipation.

[195] With the Red Handler's aversion to doorbells fresh in our memory, we understand immediately that the telephone can also cause difficulties, although, to be sure, we've also seen him answer the phone.

[196] And now our suspicions are confirmed.

[197] The author keeps the temperature cooking, the phone rings and rings, all because our protagonist is reluctant to lift the receiver and answer the call.

[198] The telephone version of a Mexican standoff.

[199] They look at each other. Understandably enough.

[200] They hope it will stop ringing. It does not stop ringing. It rings. The author shows his characters no mercy.

[201] They look at each other again.

[202] Now they look at the telephone.

[203] They go back to looking at each other.

[204] And again they turn their attention to the phone.

[205] And now they look at each other. Again. Almost as if the whole scene were lifted right out of *The Good, the Bad, and the Ugly*. ✲✲

> ✲✲ Overall I can't say I ever cared much for film, even though I would often go to the movies as a child, another one of the perks of looking much older than I was. It still tickles me to think back on the winter of 1940, when I sat in the back row masturbating in the dark to Scarlett O'Hara as she dug up radishes from the ground and took big bites out of them. Those were the days.

[206] Finally.

[207] For a second or two, we the readers think, "Here we go again."

[208] But then it's all over. The Red Handler picks up the telephone.

[209] Bernt?

[210] And if it is Bernt, who, if anyone, is he including in "we"?

[211] And here we have the difficult aunt again.

[212] The not-Red Handler also knows about the aunt. Very disturbing.

[213] This also summed up Brandeggen's feelings more and more toward the end, unfortunately.

[214] A very strong paragraph, in my opinion. I told him as much on multiple occasions.

[215] The handcuffs' being located in the bedroom is a trace of an earlier *Fifty Shades of Grey*-influenced draft. For some months in the fall of 2012, the author toyed with the idea of combining erotica with crime, hoping to maximize the novel's market potential by appealing to both genders, especially women who might be put off at the outset by some of the rougher crime elements. A closer look into sales figures and consumer demographics convinced him that erotica tended to scare men off, however, so it was too big a chance to take. Men were less willing to adjust to literature written for women, while women historically never had any choice, given the surprising amount of literature composed by men, from the perspective of men, and geared toward other men. The safest course was therefore to scrap the BDSM-based erotica—which Brandeggen had felt uncomfortable writing anyway, to say nothing of his lack of experience in that area—and instead employ the classic femme fatale and a less overt sexuality, such as we see with the woman in *The Red Handler and the Glimmer Man*. Brandeggen had intended to remove the subtle reference to BDSM in *The Red*

Handler and the Presumptuous Murderer and let the handcuffs stay in the drawer, but must have forgotten.

[216] In the *Dirty Harry* series, Clint Eastwood carried his iconic Smith & Wesson Model 29 (.44 Magnum) revolver in an identical shoulder holster from Lawman Leather.

[217] The Red Handler's methods of interrogation are again shown to be both blunt and viciously effective. We hardly even notice the punishing pressure the suspect is subjected to before he crumbles and confesses.

[218] It is impossible not to feel a certain sympathy for the culprit here; outwardly, the Red Handler seems to possess almost superhuman abilities. But inwardly, he weeps. Just like every hero. The notes to many of the Red Handler novels make much of the attention and praise our protagonist garners from the press and the town at large. We learn of his large number of admirers and of more than one stalker, all of whom function as obstacles in the novels. None of this is retained in the finished works for several reasons, as it would have made the Red Handler less believable as a character and take the focus away from the crime plot, and in *The Red Handler and the Presumptuous Murderer* specifically, it would have made the killer appear less mentally disturbed than Brandeggen intended.

[219] The Red Handler here hints that he is going to give up or simply go away. This is meant to put us on notice, as Brandeggen long considered writing a book that ended with the detective driving away from the city at dawn and leaving it all behind. There are, for instance, notes and sketches about this car ride, with light traffic in the streets and the Red Handler observing people on their way

home from parties, people standing along the road waiting for the bus, the sun creeping over the rooftops in the grayblue morning light, and garbagemen, mute and unflagging, going about their work to tidy up after the happenings in the night. All of it has to be seen in the light of Brandeggen's own fantasies about going away and escaping. Which, it must be said, he finally did.

[220] Given what we know about Brandeggen's upbringing, and everything he revealed to me over the years I knew him, this monologue shows tragic similarities to the author's own life. But it is not, alas, an isolated incident. There are many more just like them, and I took it upon myself to sit down and draw up a list:

In the evening following his son's first and only birthday party, Frode Brandeggen's father took 20% of the presents in order to teach the boy about life's unfairness, along with some vague lesson about economic trends.

For his 18th birthday, Frode Brandeggen received an exact replica of his father's promised toolbox, only much smaller and with undersized tools, so that the son would "know his place."

Brandeggen's father forbade anything that smacked of "Jesus-speak" at Christmastime and instead took his family to the mountains, where they spent on average twelve sweat-soaked hours digging snow caves. Afterward they would mark the winter solstice with a simple ceremony and conclude by looking at pictures of North Jutland beaches.

Frode Brandeggen was forced to play the cornet in the school band, but his father's undivided attention and praise were always bestowed on the tubist, who, according to Brandeggen's father, played a "man's instrument."

Brandeggen's father believed that all literature after *The Bleaching Yard* by Tarjei Vesaas was worthless. He also believed that any book published in paperback was for "spinsters and girly men."

Frode Brandeggen wanted a sibling, preferably a sister. Instead he got a print of Munch's *Crying Girl* so he could look at it and suffer guilt.

The Brandeggen family had two German Shepherds called Pain and Suffering. The boy was terrified of them both and they never hit it off, least of all on those long summer car trips in which he had to sit between the two of them in the backseat.

Frode Brandeggen was snuck into the movies as an eleven year old to watch *The Shining*, ostensibly to toughen the kid up and get him to shut up about his dream of one day going on vacation to a hotel far up in the mountains that he had seen in a newspaper ad, which he clipped out and lay under his pillow so the dream might come true. ⁑

Brandeggen's father maintained that his baldness was a direct result of his son's drawn-out birth and that this caused him to miss out on a great deal of unspecified opportunities.

Brandeggen's father held fear and guilt to be the noblest of emotions, for only through them did you really know you're alive.

Brandeggen's father was not a religious man, but insisted all the same that the universe was only six thousand years old because, as he said, anything else would've just been plain silly.

Frode Brandeggen was conceived during a quarrel. Legend has it Brandeggen's father sputtered and screamed at the decisive moment.

On two occasions, Brandeggen's father expressed the opinion that no one could consider themselves a decent person without knowing how to whittle a willow flute. He was also unwilling to teach this craft and neither the mother nor the son ever learned how to make any wind instrument whatsoever.

Brandeggen's father was unshakably convinced that doctors were no more than glorified joiners, and only the mother's persistent screams prevented the father from performing an appendectomy on his eight-year-old son, who after much gnashing of teeth was driven to the hospital.

Brandeggen's father held that the best and the only way of learning to swim was ad hoc, in situ, in deep water, without anyone swimming alongside and making things free and easy for you. Every day, over the course of two summer vacations in North Jutland, the father hurled Frode into the water, and when he one day managed to heave himself ashore with something that resembled a breaststroke, the father exclaimed: *What'd I tell you?* At this, the boy vomited. The father also believed in his peerless mastery of Latin phrases and that the minimum of a general education consisted in being able to use at least two hundred of them.

Brandeggen's father believed that every well-informed person ought to know the importance of being able to play Creedence Clearwater Revival at a high volume whenever the urge was felt, and that the time of day was of no relevance at all.

When Frode Brandeggen was seven, his father sawed a centimeter off each leg of his son's chair every day, in secret, over the course of what was likely several months, until the boy didn't even reach the edge of the table, all in order to teach his son that you must always be on your guard in life.

Brandeggen's father hated his father and believed it would build character if his son did the same.

Frode Brandeggen's mother had a lot of things she could've said. Most of it went unsaid. It was better that way.

Brandeggen's father once refused the desperate pleas of the fire brigade to move his car so that they could rescue the neighboring house that was going up in flames, because they hadn't asked "nicely."

Brandeggen's father told his son that he loved him only once, it might've been somewhere around August 1974. In any case there was some connection with Nixon's resignation.

Brandeggen's father never failed to point out, whenever the name of Adolf Hitler came up, that in spite of everything the man was famous for his love of children and dogs.

Brandeggen's father believed that suicide had to do with "knowing the time of thy visitation" and ascribed the quote to Nietzsche.

Brandeggen's father stood 1.82 meters on most days and 1.9 exactly when he was inebriated. He was often 1.9 meters tall.

Brandeggen's father, during his compulsory military service from 1965 to 1966, had been found to possess a unique ability to smell gas, even in minuscule concentrations and over long distances. He therefore considered himself indispensable to the Norwegian Armed Forces and eventually learned fluent Russian so that he could, if necessary, infiltrate the enemy and come closer to the gas facilities whose locations within the Land of the Bear he had taken it on himself to map out, a project that, to be sure, was never based on any intelligence or actual field reports, but on what he described as a highly skilled deduction and what most others described as random guesswork.

Frode Brandeggen's mother believed that tomorrow would bring a better day.

Brandeggen's father was convinced beyond doubt that he could have conducted a locomotive, and arrive at each station far more punctually than the Norwegian State Railways to boot, if only they'd given him the chance.

Brandeggen's mother had a tradition of giving her son an empty chocolate wrapper on the 1st of December before giving him the chocolate on the 24th. This was in order to teach him that the meaning of advent is waiting. On some years, his father ate the chocolate before Christmas Eve to teach the boy that all things must pass.

Brandeggen's father claimed that he knew who killed JFK and that the same people were involved in killing Olof Palme, but refused to say anything else, because the consequences would be dire if people knew the truth.

Brandeggen's father once said that no one was a grown-up before learning to lose in Ludo, and that this was meant both literally and figuratively.

Brandeggen's father told his son that Woodstock was his idea and that he and Max Yasgur had been friends for years.

Brandeggen's father said he'd beaten up both Børre Knudsen and Ludvig Nessa in 1981, in what he called the Battle of Bergeland Street.

Brandeggen's father said that he had beaten the shit out of many a man over the years, but it was beating the shit out of the yoga guru Satchidananda Saraswati with his own book, *The Healthy Vegetarian*, that had brought him the most satisfaction.

Brandeggen's father hated dancing almost as much as he hated watching others dance.

Brandeggen's father was an avid builder of Airfix model ships at a scale of 1:600 and an even-more-avid sinker of them with homemade incendiary torpedoes. The sinking of the battleship *USS Missouri* (BB-63) was at once his greatest triumph and heaviest decision; it took him three hours to get the better of himself, and he spent the night in the bathroom, surrounded by candlelight, paying respect to the miniature men who bobbed around the bathtub with microscopic life preservers around their waists. This was also the only time he was ever heard to weep openly.

Frode Brandeggen's father once described his heart as a land-fill where his family flapped about like birds scavenging for scraps.

Frode Brandeggen was born on Sunday, the 27th of September, 1970, at 2:34 in the morning. He weighed 3,560 grams. The air was thick with thunder.

Frode Brandeggen's father once considered joining the Jehovah's Witnesses for the simple reason that he could relate to people who actually looked forward to the end of the world.

Brandeggen's mother had many girlfriends in her youth. Brandeggen's father put a stop to that.

Brandeggen's father once said about Joseph Goebbels: Whatever else you might say about him, he had the gift of gab.

Frode Brandeggen's father was constipated for all of 1970 and up until the early summer of 1971. For the rest of the decade, he would mark the day of his bowel movement (June 17th) by lighting a candle in the living room and saying nothing until it had burnt all the way down, which usually lasted far into the night. By that time he was already too drunk to remember what the light represented, much less that he was the one who'd lit it.

When Brandeggen's father beat his mother, he always took care to ask her to remove her jewelry first, so that he wouldn't risk cutting himself on it.

Brandeggen's father had a hobby room, but no hobbies.

Frode Brandeggen ran away from home as a nine year old, but was located by his father near Ullandhaug Tower at 7:00 the same evening. They returned to Astra Road at 10:15 and the boy stayed home from school for eight days. In the school records he is listed as "recovering."

Brandeggen's father once opined that in any case, you couldn't fault Charles Manson for his taste in music.

Brandeggen's father never went to parent-teacher conferences. He simply never did.

Frode Brandeggen hated his name, like everyone who wishes they were somebody else.

Frode Brandeggen's mother worked as a grocery-store cashier and during her breaks she would talk to her coworkers in great detail about vacations that she'd never actually been on. To herself, she justified this by saying this was the cheapest and indeed the only way of going places.

Brandeggen's father viewed pilots as the bus drivers of the sky and never doubted for a second in his ability to land a 747, if only they'd given him the chance.

For many years Brandeggen's father kept the following in his closet: a Mauser Model B rifle, a Krag-Jørgensen M/1894, a Winchester 1500 shotgun, a Russian Makarov pistol, a Luger, an AG3, and loads of ammunition. This was common knowledge and something he constantly reminded everyone about.

Brandeggen's father had a recurring dream that it was he who'd set fire to the Reichstag, and that he later hit it big in the matchstick industry.

Brandeggen's father once grabbed one of his son's teachers by the throat at a Christmas party because the teacher had written Henrik Wergeland's name with a V.

As the years went by, it emerged that Brandeggen's father hated the following: wadmal, hedgehogs, earmuffs, shower curtains, soap bubbles, macramé, the periodic table, fake fur, drop-in visits, dental floss, all types of wood except birch (mahogany and hickory made him especially furious), enameled pots and utensils, rubber duckies, fabric softeners, footstools, elephants and several other threatened species, the spring equinox, *Life of Pi*, damp kitchen towels, asbestos, church bells, children, toothpaste, phone numbers, robes in general but especially bathrobes, toothpicks, matches, slippers, bicycles, public and private fountains, doors, Ziploc bags, hair, adventures, America, chests, reggae, snow, photography equipment, copper plates, sailing ships, the color blue, the price of electricity, Boy and Girl Scouts, 4-H and all types of track and field, cords and plugs, cream, luggage with wheels, currency, ice hockey, all types of flooring, contact lenses, backpacks, the port authority, plastics, onions, office landscapes, tennis balls, denim, New Year's fireworks, screws, the sale of groceries by weight, scaffolding, gymnastics, cardboard boxes, wallpaper, washing machines, garbage dumps, shirt buttons, ladders, navels, piña colada, honeymoons, open flame, traffic jams and gridlock in general, handbags, dialysis, magnifying glasses, basements, postmen, magnets, monsters, flip flops, sing-alongs, the sea, death, love, Acquired Immune Deficiency Syndrome, the Yuppie era, sunglasses, future prospects, reusable shopping bags, sculptures, ships in a bottle, folding screens, screw-on lids, freeze-dried coffee, fecal matter, feathers, disco, discos, photocopiers, legal hearings, wrestling, the weather, every kind of bag, driving schools, the police, Saint John's Fire, protective footwear, canaries, the moon, long lists, clogs, the government, mammon, steeplechases, roller coasters, swings, trampolines and sandboxes; practically all humans, playsets, Easter, the suburbs, mailboxes, bric-à-brac, chess, seatbelts, fashion magazines, ginger, plastic bags, bowler hats, mints, winter, summer, fall, spring, Mondays, tealights, fractions, downlights, bay windows, cigarettes, bedwetting, barns, pants pockets, Napoleon, plane tickets, Mount Everest, female program announcers, fish without gills, newspapers in Berliner format, tinsel, lawn sprinklers, mildew, lawnmowers, parents, concentration camps, chlorophyll, wooden huts, swimming caps, panic attacks, sixpences, saunas, nature, covered cheese dishes, drypoint and woodcut, dog whistles, flypaper, nailclippers, stages along a journey, shortcuts, detours, fun times, muesli, urinary tract infections, pancakes, carrom, computers, dandelions, cymbals, stairs, freckles, art, opening hours, prostheses, Tupperware, all marine life, knife handles, potpourri, Westerns, applause, restraining orders, envelopes, snakeskin, oscillators, footnotes, moss, doorsills, garden fences, parasols, hippies, the Red Cross, coincidences, soccer fields, grandfather clocks plus all timers and alarm clocks, chemistry sets, running shoes, grand opening sales, junk mail, wrenches, clothes racks, movables. But none of these did he hate anywhere near as much as Christmas.

According to the stamp on the library card, Frode Brandeggen's mother borrowed Doug Richmond's *How to Disappear Completely and Never Be Found* from the Stavanger Public Library on May 12, 1986, and returned it a week later.

"The most important thing my father taught me," said Brandeggen's father on one occasion, "is to be economical with your punches so that you don't tire yourself."

Frode Brandeggen's father paid no taxes between 1972 and 1983, nor in any of the years following.

Frode Brandeggen's father could recite the entire film *The Sorrow and the Pity* from memory, and after some years, so could Frode Brandeggen.

Brandeggen's father said enthusiastically of the Manhattan Project: "It was no child's play, that's for sure!"

Frode Brandeggen's father promised to stop drinking the day he was no longer thirsty.

Brandeggen's father said: "If I had a motorcycle, I'd roar out of this fucking shittown for good." Brandeggen's father was unusually consumed with the importance of a good exit. Again, some Nietzsche thing.

Frode Brandeggen's father regarded himself as the foremost authority on *Sonderkommandos* in Norway and believed he could have written a brilliant thesis on the subject, if only they'd given him the chance.

Brandeggen's father once said of Pol Pot that the man, if nothing else, was a go-getter.

Like Colargol the bear, Brandeggen's father was able to hum in both major and minor keys.

Brandeggen's father once said of Beckett's *Waiting for Godot*, after being unwillingly dragged to the theater to see it with his wife: "I could've written that myself. If only they'd given me the chance."

Brandeggen's father made the following laconic observation: "The way people are dismembered by chainsaw in the movies is unrealistic, the cuts are much too smooth. In reality they'd be jagged and uneven, because the tissue is soft and the body exerts no counterpressure."

Brandeggen's father was generally an admirer of the Nicaraguan Contras and claimed to be in possession of a copy of *Operaciones psicológicas enurdoa de guerrillas*, signed by Enrique Bermúdez and Ayn Rand.

Brandeggen's father dreamed of being a gardener. When he woke up, he pushed it out of mind.

Brandeggen's father eagerly read other people's mail if the chance presented itself, and the chance presented itself surprisingly often.

Frode Brandeggen's father proudly claimed never to have made dinner. "Never!"

Brandeggen's father clung to the idea that he primarily snuck alcohol home from Jutland in order to contribute to the Norwegian GDP by keeping the customs agents busy and on their toes. He held them in a strange, loathing respect.

Over time, Frode Brandeggen's mother became so careful that she washed everything on delicate cycle.

Frode Brandeggen's father was present at four autopsies in their entirety at the Stavanger Central Hospital by presenting himself as a researcher for a Polish documentary producer. According to him, he did this because he wanted to "see if people were as rotten on the inside as they are on the outside."

Brandeggen's father expressed disappointment at the fact that he was never suspected of being the Unabomber. "There's no reason it couldn't have been me, if only they'd given me the chance."

Frode Brandeggen's father died suddenly and dramatically of a heart attack on a nameless North Jutland beach as his son was being buried in Stavanger. His last words are said to be, "Oh, dear God, dear God."

⁑ Brandeggen repeatedly specifies in his papers that he wants the title *The Red Handler* to appear in the same hand-drawn typeface used on the posters for *The Shining* and for the individual novel titles to appear in the same variant of Helvetica used in the film's intertitles, a desire that was granted by Gyldendal Norsk Forlag. ⊗ Whether or not this has to do with this specific event is uncertain.

⊗ The typeface and poster for *The Shining* were created by the graphic designer Saul Bass, whose film posters included *The Man with the Golden Arm* (1955), *Love in the Afternoon* (1957), *Bonjour Tristesse* (1958), *Vertigo* (1958), *Anatomy of a Murder* (1959), *The Magnificent Seven* (1960), *Bunny Lake is Missing* (1965), and the opening titles for *The Seven Year Itch*, *North by Northwest* (1959), *Psy-*

cho (1960), *Spartacus* (1960), *Ocean's 11* (1960) and *West Side Story* (1961). The extent of Brandeggen's familiarity with Bass's body of work is unknown. In general, and curiously—given the pains he took to specify the typeface for the novels—Brandeggen was adamant that authors and filmmakers should never concern themselves with the works' visual appearance or other (as he put it) "base, commercial aspects," which served only as distractions from the artist's real work, the text, the images. ⊄

⊄ Therefore, Brandeggen categorically refused to take any stance on the cover designs that Gyldendal presented him prior to the publication of *Conglomeratic Breath*. The designer, Meilein Bakke Tungland, is said to have attempted to call him several times to discuss the sketches, only for the author time and again to hang up on her as soon as he realized what the call was about. None of this prevented Brandeggen from subsequently expressing his dissatisfaction with the final result, and for years he bore a considerable grudge toward the designer for what he called "her po-mo hipster streak," which he believed had ruined the cover and with it much of his book's commercial potential. "This is a dreadful dust jacket," he said to his editor. ∅ "Absolutely dreadful. It would've been far better to have used an oil painting, preferably something by Hertervig." ∅∅

Ø Brandeggen was consistent in his use of the term *dust jacket*. In this area he belonged to the old school.

ØØ Brandeggen held the Stavanger painter Lars Hertervig (1830–1902) in as high regard as the poet Sigbjørn Obstfelder (1866–1900, also from Stavanger), and he loved Obstfelder as much as he despised the author Alexander L. Kielland (1849–1906, also from Stavanger). Around the time he finished *Conglomeratic Breath*, he scribbled a few ideas for a biographical novel on Hertervig and the painter's mental illness, only to become enraged when the far more successful Jon Fosse released the novels *Melancholy* and *Melancholy II* in 1995 and 1996, a pair of biographical novels about Hertervig that centered upon the painter's mental illness. Brandeggen therefore shifted his focus to Obstfelder with a sketch for an intense, taut biographical novel about the angst-ridden, pining poet, only to experience a fresh blow and another bout of rage when the Stavanger author Einar O. Risa published the novel *L. C. Nielsen* in 2000, a biographical novel about none other than Sigbjørn

Obstfelder. The novels, Brandeggen
had to admit, were exceptional.

[221] *Everyone you arrest is yourself. And don't you forget it.* Though
the Red Handler may not hear this, the author is talking equally
to himself now, and if it wasn't apparent before, now the veil is
lifted to reveal just how personal this project is for Frode Brandeggen. He knows the end is approaching as he writes these
words; he knows he can never outrun himself, and he knows
it is as impossible to hide all his baggage within an impenetrable labyrinth like *Conglomeratic Breath* as it is to throw it
all overboard in the Red Handler universe. Banalist literature,
the turn to crime writing, the idea of a punk-inspired rebellion against the commercial literati who look the other way on
artistic quality so long as there's money to be made: despite all
this, he never manages to rid himself of himself and, thereby,
free himself. Rage, despair, and disappointment all end in sheer
resignation, leading both Brandeggen and the Red Handler to
give up. There's no place to go, no place to run off to anymore.
What was intended as a hard-hitting polemic, with commercial
potential to boot, ends with a whimper. ⁎⁎ This might be why I
persist in my dogged admiration for these books, and why I've
decided that this will be my final annotation project; it's less
that the literary quality is especially superior to anything else
I've worked on, than the fact that these books are the result of
this one little human's struggle. He gave it everything he'd got,
and failed. That's how he viewed it, in any case. There is really
something quite beautiful about it, this defeat. And that is why
I will always do my part to safeguard it.

⁎⁎ Brandeggen regarded the Sex Pistols album, *Never
Mind the Bollocks—Here's the Sex Pistols,* as the clearest

example of how genuine rebellion could coexist with commercial appeal/earnings potential. Coming from an avant-gardist tradition—however much the Red Handler project was conceived as revenge or protest—he also, as we now know, intended it as an artistic trojan horse, since a part of him genuinely believed it had real literary merit while also giving people what they (didn't know they) wanted. Even avant-gardists dream of garnering followers. Otherwise, they're just avant.

[222] Many readers will react negatively to the plot of this novel, since the transgression hardly warrants more than a warning (if that). A warning which, moreover, the Red Handler has no authority to issue. But this novel is crucial to understanding the Red Handler/Brandeggen's breakdown, the seeds of which are visible in this sudden inability to distinguish between serious criminality and insignificant breaches of social convention.

[223] This novel may have been inspired by Red Plum Bladder (*Taphrina pruni*), a fungal disease afflicting the red plum tree, causing the fruit to grow elongated and up to ten times its normal size, in resemblance to a bladder. This novel likewise comprises the Red Handler series' turning point: our usually so stalwart detective overreacts to an accident involving urine, far exceeding his mandate. As readers we almost hear something snap within the detective, but are powerless to do anything but follow him through the downward spiral we see in the rest of this novel and the two remaining, *The Red Handler Comes Too Late* and *The Red Handler Lands in Trouble with the Authorities*.

[224] Another hidden reference to parkour.

[225] Setup. Payoff. Perfect.

[226] And that is exactly what is about to happen. Not hard to imagine this as a sentence equally directed at Brandeggen himself.

[227] The Red Handler knows his private detective law and takes no chances.

[228] There is really something beautiful and almost utopian about this Red Handler world in which it is possible—to an extent— to trust the criminals.

[229] Always. Brandeggen knew this better than anyone, unfortunately.

[230] There is nothing wrong with the choice of a good lavender soap.

[231] As we know, he wasn't unacquainted with disappointment either, Brandeggen.

[232] Among the few things I remember sharing a laugh with him over, people's perpetual disappointment with the weather in Stavanger stands out.

[233] Another reference to Copenhagen. As if Brandeggen lives a double life, two totally irreconcilable existences. Also a reference to his family, about whom we learn nothing, apart from scattered references to the aunt.

[234] As with Brandeggen.

235 Glenn Gould was the hypochondriac who was proven right in the end. His many ailments were a constant source of worry for him, and he kept a detailed log of his own blood pressure. Gould died after a stroke that occurred on September 27th, 1982, two days after his 50th birthday. Three thousand people attended his funeral. By comparison, thirteen attended Brandeggen's.

236 Cliff Eastwood (born Blagorodna "Blago" Lazarov, 1962) had a relatively short career, with *Зелени шуми, сини панталони. Целосни луѓе и деца* [Green Forests, Blue Pants. Whole People and Children, 1984] marking his high point as an artist, a sentimental Macedonian tale of Yugoslavia at the end of the 60s. Other films include *Те бакнувам. Потоа морам да одам на работа* [I'll Kiss You, But Then I've Got to Go to Work, 1980], *Вечерва* [Tonight, 1979], the comedy *Остеопорозата не е за слаби души* [Osteoporosis Isn't for the Faint of Heart, 1983] and the British erotic thriller-comedy *My Genes in Your Jeans* (1984). *Ŝancoj de doloro en la lando de murdo* [The Threat of Pain in the Land of Murder, 1985] was Eastwood's last. He was killed in the spring of 1986 during the filming of *Збогум Тито* [Farewell, Tito] when he accidentally stepped backward into the tail rotor of a helicopter that had just landed on the set. ⁑ According to the biography, *Овек во илјадници парчиња* [Man in a Thousand Bits, 1989], Cliff Eastwood had never seen any Clint Eastwood movies. ⊗

⁑ Exactly as the Ukrainian director Boris Sagal had done exactly five years to the day, outside the Timberline Lodge in Oregon (the same hotel whose exterior Stanley Kubrick used for *The Shining*, 1980). Apart from that, Sagal's most famous work as a director was *The Omega Man* (1971).

⊗ Cliff Eastwood is also the man behind the legendary Dylan-inspired hit "Hey, Mr. Mandolin Man" (Beograd Fanci Records, 1981), originally a saccharine tune about homesickness that gained new life and significance in 1992 when paramilitary Chetniks embraced it and deliberately misread it as heralding Milošević's speech on the Kosovo plain in 1987 and as a defense of Republika Srpska. Unconfirmed sources also have it that the song was used internally as a song of praise to Ratko Mladić, known in Western media as the Butcher of Bosnia, but among his countrymen as the Mandolin, ostensibly because of his unparalleled virtuosity when he, whether in moments of carousal or extreme rage, took to the instrument and belted out a few tunes. "Hey, Mr. Mandolin Man" was the only song Eastwood recorded in his lifetime.

[237] As it happens, there is no *Kvalito Premion* prize, nor any special festival for Esperanto films in Eastern Europe (though there is one in Brazil), but Leslie Stevens (1924–1998) was a very real person and it is striking that Brandeggen a) incorporates a reference to one of the film directors/artists he most admired and b) doesn't also devote more space to him. In the years between *Conglomeratic Breath* and the Red Handler project, Brandeggen also worked on a critical biography of this American director, producer, and screenwriter. Stevens, born in Washington D.C. to a well-off family of high-ranking naval officers, decided early on not to follow in the family footsteps. At fifteen he ran away from home. He sold his play, *The Mechanical Rat*, to Orson Welles's Mercury Theater and joined the touring theater troupe. In 1942 he enlisted in

the Air Force, at twenty the youngest captain in the American military. In Greenwich Village he briefly formed half of a song-and-dance duo whose other member was Joseph Stefano, later known for writing the screenplay to Hitchcock's *Psycho*. At twenty-two, he worked the night shift at a Manhattan hotel, and at twenty-five ran the same shift at a psychiatric hospital. He tried his hand at many different jobs. He didn't talk about all of them. The year 1955 saw the premiere of Stevens's first Broadway production, *The Champagne Complex*, a light comedy about a girl with an uncontrollable urge to get undressed every time she drinks champagne. The play ran for twenty-three performances before closing. His next play, 1956's lavishly-produced *The Lovers*, was a period drama based on the notion of *droit du seigneur* from the Middle Ages. ⁑ The *New York Times* hailed it as a "work of art," while the *New York Post* described it as "dramatically ineffective." *The Lovers* was taken off the marquee after four performances. His first Broadway success came in 1958 with *The Marriage-Go-Round*, about a Swedish beauty who complicates the lives of a married couple in academia when she asks to be impregnated by the man to conceive a child with his brain and her looks. Stevens, having finally been brought in from the cold by Broadway, decided to go out west and try his chances in Hollywood. One of his first projects was the screenplay to Arthur Penn's *The Left-Handed Gun* (1958), based on Gore Vidal's teleplay that imagined Billy the Kid as a homosexual in deep denial of his true identity. In 1960, Stevens got the chance to write and direct his first feature, *Private Property*, a new-wave crime film with erotic undertones (prompting the Catholic Church to condemn the film on moral grounds), with Ted McCord as cinematographer (whose credits included *The Treasure of Sierra Madre*, *East of Eden*, and *The Sound of Music*), filmed over the course of ten days primarily at the homes of Stevens and his neighbor. *Private Property* was initially denied the seal of the Production Code by the American film censors and therefore failed to obtain a distributor. It was considered a lost film until 1994. Among contemporary reviews, the *New Yorker* called the acting "uniformly terrible" and *Film Quarterly* dismissed the film as thinly-veiled pornography and an insult to women everywhere. One positive review praised it as a "harrowing and extended clinical picture of physical, sexual, and mental violation." Even more curious than these reviews, however, is the reaction of Jacqueline Kennedy after she and John F. Kennedy attended a private screening the same evening as the decisive 1960 Democratic primary contest in West Virginia. She called it "some awful, sordid thing about some murder in California—really, I mean, just morbid" that left her and John "terribly depressed," a mood that quickly lifted at the news of the primary victory. Brandeggen's interest in Stevens can be traced first and foremost back to *Incubus* (1966), a film which prompted Brandeggen to become a fluent speaker of Esperanto. Shot by Conrad Hall (whose three Oscars for cinematography include one for *Butch Cassidy and the Sundance Kid*), *Incubus* is a black and white horror flick starring a pre-*Star Trek* William Shatner. The language in the film is Esperanto, or at least a very poorly pronounced Esperanto, as general consensus would have it. Brandeggen wholeheartedly agreed with this consensus. The film's use of Esperanto—as unusual for its time as it would be today *﹡﹡﹡*—was, according to Stevens, a deliberate strategy to evoke the uncanny, and he forbade the dubbing of the film into any other language. In recent decades it has emerged—much as Brandeggen himself thought—that the film was made in Esperanto also in the expectation that it would lead to a greater international audience once Esperanto caught on around the world.

Incubus takes place in a fictional country town called Nomen Tuum (Latin: Your Name), whose central attraction is a well that heals the sick and makes people beautiful. This cosmetic side-effect attracts a rather corrupt demographic who then fall victim to the demons and the darkness lurking on the outskirts of the town. I won't devote any more space to the banal and often confusing plot. For our purposes it suffices to mention the Baphomet/Omega-like goat that the titular incubus summons in the final sequence in the town cathedral, given its possible resonance with the Ω value and "the presence of absolute Negativity" (see note 19). Noah Moslex's film *Doctor Omega* (1986) also

contains a nod to Leslie Stevens in the end credits, and Brandeggen's extensive 142-page notes to *The Red Handler Stumbles across It* mention the last scene of *Incubus* several times. It is in these notes we find out that Brandeggen saw *Incubus* for the first time during his treatment at ███████████████████ ██████████████████, where he and a female fellow patient happened upon the film in the employee breakroom and stole it before the employee who'd rented it could return it to the video store. In the notes, Brandeggen relates how within a few weeks he and a few other unnamed patients had secretly obtained a VCR and TV and, through an elaborate smoke-and-mirrors scheme, began a nightly screening of the film in the institution's basement/gymnasium without the employees' knowledge, such that in time the film "was popular and very meaningful to us, to put it mildly." Furthermore, the Stevens/Brandeggen connection is even more fascinating given their similar career paths and the consequences that followed. Like Brandeggen, Stevens was unquestionably talented, but the quest to combine artistic impulse with a mass appeal led both men far out to sea, where

there was no lighthouse to help navigate back. It is exactly this self-imposed disconnect from the world, whether from the industry or fellow colleagues, which comprises both their courage and their hubris. When the realization hits them that they've gone too far, it arouses a not-inconsiderable degree of panic and rage, which in turn finds expression in an unconventional style and, whether consciously or no, a drift toward artistic self-destruction. *Incubus*, to some extent, can therefore be seen as Red-Handlerism par excellence. Stevens aims to create his own space where he can reach out to people (by way of Esperanto) and simultaneously run the whole venture aground (again, by way of Esperanto). And at this point I can't help but mention the elephant in the room: that Brandeggen's micronovel project was doomed from the start, a bit like the high jumper who pulls back mid-jump, resulting in an inconsistent style; the Red Handler novels, for all their sharply truncated length, seem at times needlessly long. While, for instance, *The Red Handler Hot on the Trail* is exemplarily compact and quickly lays out the exposition, conflict, rising action (confined to the sentence: "The Red Handler burst out of his vehicle"), and resolution ("Before the thief could protest, the Red Handler had laid him out, smack on the ground"), *The Red Handler and the Great Diamond Heist* is marred by long, irrelevant passages and details that have little to do with the story, but are present partly for the resonance with Brandeggen's own history, partly because he lost sight of compactness and other ground rules of Banalism, or perhaps also because he, like Stevens, thought he was able to build a bridge between the Red Handler project, with its distillations, and a more expansive, detail-fixated literature of which *Conglomeratic Breath* was the disastrous representative. Other novels, like *The Red Handler and the Musical Bandit*, are not altogether encumbered by inessentials, and yet they depart from the aim of compactness, the almost clinical exposition-conflict-resolution model; all too often, Brandeggen falls for the temptation to add descriptive, suspense-heightening elements that make the novel resemble, at least in some ways, any run-of-the-mill crime novel. Which it decidedly isn't. The novel is in stark contrast to the subsequent, more restrained *The Red Handler and the Secret Massage Studio*, where not a word is wasted and which seems almost a corrective to its predecessor. But that doesn't last, for *The Red Handler and the Unsolvable Mystery of the Burmese Cat* and *The Red Handler and the Difficult Sabbath* are both astonishingly long. Their divergence from one of Brandeggen's maxims ("Life is short, but not short enough") seems paradoxical. One fully understandable response would be to criticize the Red Handler novels for their varying lengths, for the way they start to sprawl out in different directions. But while all these objections (and a good many others, God knows) are understandable, it is possible to look at it all from another angle, from which the novels, for all their defects, all their failures, become organic; Brandeggen's literature comes alive. Through his inability to force the novels into a schematic and compact system, he shows himself time and again to be, well, human. This was the best he could do under the conditions he was working under. He was a man left shipwrecked by writing, but write he did. He worked at it. Many an author will write one book and then spend the rest of their lives talking about all the books they're going to write. Not Brandeggen. He wrote, and he did so under a growing disengagement from the world, hemmed in by disappointment with himself, growing more and more afraid of the black dog that had moved in with him to stay. The Red Handler is his farewell to everything, Brandeggen's last word to the world. I believe he hated writing these books, and at the same time he loved it. And perhaps we see in these novels, especially the ones that explode their formal limits, traces of the enjoyment that led him to start writing in the first place. This enjoyment, if that is the right word, is what lies hidden in the confrontational language he drew from Walter Hopping's Banalist prose (particularly *Garbled Love* [1972] and *Evol Garbage* [1974], Dalkey Archive) and William D. Lindquist's *Hear Me Out: Language in the Time of Deaf Ears* (Oxford University Press, 2004). The clear references to *Evol Garbage* in many of the Red Handler novels convinced Gyldendal's Editor in Chief Kari Marstein and Fiction Editor Harald Ofstad Fougner to give Brandeggen the benefit of the doubt and publish the novels posthumously when I sent them the manuscripts I recovered from Brandeggen's belongings, as did the notes and the letter to me, which stipulated the novels could only be published if accompanied by my annotations, without editing or interference of any kind from the publisher. A stipulation to which Gyldendal Norsk Forlag (after a time, to be sure) assented.

⁂ Up until the start of the eighteenth century, the notion of *droit du seigneur* was (allegedly) related to the right of a landowner or feudal lord to spend the wedding night with the bride when one of his subjects got married.

⁂⁎ The first film to use Esperanto as its main language was *Angoroj* (1964). *Incubus* was the second.

[238] The word "belonged" in this sentence is worth noting. Brandeggen was adamant that an unwritten, but binding form of belonging not only applied to church (which he never attended) or school, but to many other places as well: the hair salon, grocery store, bus stop, pharmacy, doctor's or dentist's office,

liquor store, and so on. For Brandeggen it was unthinkable, for instance, to go to a different hairdresser than the one he had visited for the first time once he was old enough to choose where to get his hair cut. Regardless of whether the salon was in his neighborhood or a different one, regardless of whether the business moved to a different location or the owners closed it down before opening a similar one elsewhere, his affective ties obliged him to continue having his hair done in the place where he felt he "belonged." He also kept using the same bus stop, even many years after a new one was installed in an area that would have cut his walking distance by half. He spent a lot of time getting around to the various places he belonged, to do whatever errands needed doing.

[239] The Red Handler's aversion to answering the phone is duly related in *The Red Handler and the Presumptuous Murderer.*

[240] The mental toll and ramifications from the Red Handler's overreaction to the offense in *The Red Handler and the Out-of-Control Urine* are on full display here.

[241] As did Brandeggen.

[242] A clear reference to the Swedish poet Gunnar Ekelöf and his collection *Late on Earth* (1932). Ekelöf occupied a special place in Brandeggen's heart, and the line *give me poison to die or dreams to live* from this collection served almost as a life motto for the tormented Norwegian author. He was also fond of the collection *Non Serviam* (1945), with its declaration: *I am a stranger in this country / but this country is no stranger in me! / I am not at home in this country / but this country feigns a home in me!* For Brandeggen the words probably expressed something of

his entire outlook on life. In the final letter I received from him, some weeks after he visited me in Dresden, early that spring, he enclosed a poem from Ekelöf's *Ferry Song* (1941), with the last two lines underlined: *I believe in the lonesome human / in her the lonesome wanderer / not running as the dog to its own scent / not fleeing as the wolf from man's scent / at once human and antihuman. // Where is communion to be found? / Take flight on the high, outer road: / The cattle in others are the cattle in you. / Walk on the low, inner road: / What's at the bottom in you is at the bottom in others. / Hard to get used to yourself. / Hard to be cured of yourself. // She who does so shall never be outcast. / She who does so shall always remain in solidarity. / <u>Only the impractical is practical / in the long run</u>.*

[243] This paragraph is an offshoot from an early phase of Brandeggen's work on the Red Handler, presumably around 2004 to 2005, when Brandeggen was exploring the possibility of writing the books as science fiction. Inspired by Stanislaw Lem, the Strugatsky brothers, Øyvind Rimbereid's *Solaris Corrected*, and not least Philip K. Dick, he outlined a series under the working title of *Pink Radiation/2-3-74*. The idea involved the Red Handler (here called ArSiGa) patrolling the streets of a future dystopian version of Stavanger, in which the city has grown to over a million residents due to the oil industry, whose greed, however, has transformed some parts of the city into refineries. Crude oil and toxic waste flow through the streets under a sky of perpetual darkness, where dark-blue clouds allow only faint glimmers of the sun to shine through. In the only book for which Brandeggen completed a first draft, *Randa Simulacrum Malignum*, ArSiGa wakes up in his apartment at Kalhammaren and looks out over the fjord, where the newest oil rigs are lined up close together, ready to be towed to sea. ArSiGa goes deep into the slums of Randaberg (called *Randa* in the text) to fight

crime and help the lost. Brandeggen leans heavily on Dick's *The Unteleported Man* (1966) and has ArSiGa teleport the people he arrests to a penal colony on Neptune's moon Triton, from which they can never return. We assume. At the same time, ArSiGa becomes more and more entangled in the illegal teleportation of Randa slumdwellers to the affluent moon, Titan (which revolves around Saturn), where local legislation requires everyone arriving autonomously to the Elips Island reception center (which is also where all well-off migrants from the massive, regularly-running Gargantua ships are processed before being transported on to their new abode) shall be taken care of, given a home and a job, and receive the same treatment and privileges as the rest of the population. A body of laws that, one should add, were created in a time before teleporting was invented and which are now the subject of heated debate on Earth as well as Titan. The same laws apply, moreover, to Triton, where every new arrival becomes a prisoner for life, which is complicated by the teleport device used by ArSiGa and certain others, an early, off-market prototype with an 82%–7% success rate. This means that the teleporting fails 18% of the time, in which 11% of the persons are sent nowhere, and 7% are sent to the wrong end station; slumdwellers who are on their way to a new start on Titan, in other words, end up at the penal colony on Triton, while Triton-destined criminals arrive at Titan, where they not only get the chance to continue their shady activities, but also the opportunity to return to Earth, this time with new identities and under the guise of being well-heeled Titanites. Complications ensue. Exactly why Brandeggen abandoned *Randa Simulacrum Malignum* is uncertain, but it might be because the work ran the risk of becoming too complex and he feared, as he put it, "getting lost in the same woods where I found *Conglomeratic Breath*," or because it coincided with his discovery of Walter

Hopping's Banalist prose, which led Brandeggen down a different, less obstacle-strewn path.

[244] The use of profanity here, and the highly emotional charge to words like, "What tragedy," at the end of the previous paragraph, point toward a crimefighting hero and an author beginning to bend under the pressure of an unrelenting journey through the dark labyrinths of crime. It never ends.

[245] How many different ways this sentence could be read.

[246] Frode Brandeggen's only source of news was the local daily *Rogalands Avis*, which he detested. He held it to be one of Norway's worst newspapers, which for him was reason enough to keep subscribing. It helped him start the day with a certain boost, knowing that yet another edition awaited on his doorstep to grumble about. Myself, I subscribe to *Süddeutsche Zeitung*, *Die Tageszeitung, Neues Deutschland, Junge Welt, Der Freitag, Der Spiegel, konkret, Sächsische Zeitung, Star Tribune, The Boston Globe, The Washington Post, Le Monde, The Guardian, Asahi Shimbun*, and *Sports Hochi*. And in recent years, *Rogalands Avis*, for the same reasons as Brandeggen. It comes to me a day late, as if to amplify my irritation.

[247] It is almost hard to stomach, the way Brandeggen in so few words creates sympathy for the Red Handler's archnemesis, the Glimmer Man, making us feel guilty for "illicitly" wanting to learn more about the Glimmer Man and his struggle in the shadow of the great Red Handler. Add to it the reference to the Glimmer Man's utter disregard for his own safety, much as Brandeggen previously portrayed the Red Handler in *The Red Handler Stumbles across It*.

[248] The reference to Kaddish and minyan has resonance with *The Red Handler and the Difficult Sabbath*—as well as Brandeggen's idea that everything might be easier, or at least easier to make sense of, if he were Jewish. "Happiness is a good rabbi," he often said. And with that I can only nod in agreement.

[249] The notion of the last word here is important, as is the symbolism in the fact that it is the Glimmer Man, and not Brandeggen's alter ego, the Red Handler, who has the honor of concluding here and ushering in the silence. As an author, Brandeggen believed it necessary to work toward a point where he had no more to say, or rather, had no more need of writing. A literary terminus, marked by textual stasis.

[250] This sentence is nowhere in any of Brandeggen's notes or drafts, but was added to the manuscript by hand.

[251] The rest of the text is presumably nonexistent. Why Brandeggen chose to put his pen down, or simply was unable to finish the final novel in the series, we have not the faintest clue. One possibility, of course, which we cannot immediately rule out, is that the novel was never meant to be any longer, but rather, in keeping with the series' guiding concept, a narrative whose masterfully abrupt cliffhanger ending jumps straight ahead to the final climax, where the infamy of the authorities' interference in and strangulation of the Red Handler's career becomes all too apparent, without making us get through hundreds of pages of inessential detail first. The Red Handler is taken out of commission at last, not by the criminal underground, but by the very institutions that ought to have stood by him in his enterprise. Oh, the irony. The incomplete sentence also enshrines a shocking truth: The Red Handler sits still. Unmoving. Para-

lyzed? Perhaps. Resigned? Not impossible. Aware that the authorities are ready to knock on his door at any time and lay him flat against the wall under this or that pretext? Absolutely. And then, the word at the end: *and. And*, pointing toward something of which neither the Red Handler nor the reader has any idea. *And*, denoting some awful, unnamable future thing. Or maybe, *and* in the sense of something else out there, a hopeful glimpse of a whole new life altogether. Maybe that's what it means. I, for one, like to think that it does.

252 Blah blah blah.

Ω

The introductory and concluding epigraphs *That there* ... and *I'm not here* ... are taken from the song *How to Disappear Completely* by Radiohead. Thanks to aøo, ss, gc, jr, km, te, gh, rs, jbc, mh. Etc.

JOHAN HARSTAD (b. 1979 in Stavanger) is a Norwegian author and playwright. He made his debut in 2001 with the short prose collection *Herfra blir du bare eldre* (*From Here on in You Just Get Older*) and have since published collections of short stories, plays, the YA novel *172 Hours on The Moon* (2008) as well as the novels *Buzz Aldrin, What Happened to You in All the Confusion?* (2005), *Hässelby* (2007) and *Max, Mischa & The Tet Offensive* (2015). He was the in-house playwright at the National Theater in Oslo in 2009 and both his own plays and plays based on his books have been produced in several European countries. For the production of *Osv.* (*Etc.*) at the National Theatre, Harstad was awarded the Ibsen Prize. In 2017, he received the Hunger Prize for his "younger, eminent" literary work, and the following year, he was awarded the Dutch Europese Literatuurprijs for his 1,100-page novel *Max, Mischa & the Tet Offensive*, which has received overwhelming acclaim in Norway, Denmark, Germany and the Netherlands. In 2019 Harstad was awarded the prestigious Svenska Akademiens Dobloug Award for his authorship. His books have been published in over 30 countries. Harstad lives in Oslo.

DAVID M. SMITH translates Norwegian fiction and has an MFA in literary translation from the University of Iowa.